DAY OF JUDGMENT

**Center Point
Large Print**

**This Large Print Book carries the
Seal of Approval of N.A.V.H.**

WAYNE D. OVERHOLSER

DAY OF JUDGMENT

CENTER POINT PUBLISHING

THORNDIKE, MAINE

This Center Point Large Print edition
is published in the year 2003 by arrangement with
Golden West Literary Agency.

The text of this Large Print edition is unabridged. In other
aspects, this book may vary from the original edition. Printed in
Thailand. Set in 16-point Times New Roman type by
Bill Coskrey and Gary Socquet.

ISBN 1-58547-267-0

Library of Congress Cataloging-in-Publication Data.

Overholser, Wayne D., 1906-
    Day of judgment / Wayne D. Overholser.--Center Point large print ed.
        p. cm.
    ISBN 1-58547-267-0 (lib. bdg. : alk. paper)
    1. Large type books. I. Title.

PS3529.V33 D38 2003
813'.54--dc21

                                                    2002073918

ONE

AS Kirby Grant watched the wagon train complete its curling motion into a circle on the east bank of Cherry Creek, he told himself he had never in the world expected everyone to get here. More than a hundred people had left Linn County, Kansas, on August 25, 1860. They had angled northwest until they struck the Kaw and then had turned west, taking the Smoky Hill route to the Pikes Peak mining country. Now they were only fifteen miles out of Denver, and every man, woman and child who had started was here within an easy day's travel of their destination.

Dave Thorn, captain of the wagon train, reined his big black in beside Kirby's buckskin. He said, "We're here."

Kirby laughed. "I was just thinking the same. I sure didn't think we'd all make it."

Thorn was a blocky man with a salt-and-pepper spade beard. He carried himself with quiet dignity. Not once to Kirby's knowledge had he lost his temper in more than six hundred miles of travel. They had faced Indian danger, torrential prairie storms had struck them, and along the western end of the trail they'd made dry camps more than once, but Thorn had never given the slightest hint that he feared they would not reach their destination.

He was an experienced plainsman, so he had known what to do when they faced danger. When they had failed to find water, he had ordered the men to dig shallow wells in the sandy bottoms of the dry stream beds and they'd had enough water to survive. He was a born leader of men, it seemed to Kirby, and he was even more respected at this moment than he'd been the morning they'd left Linn County.

Thorn was fifty years old; he had the best of health, a wonderful wife, and enough money to get started out here in the mining country. He would, Kirby thought, go a long way in a new territory where leadership was needed.

"I suppose some of 'em will wonder why we're corralling tonight now that we're almost there," Thorn said worriedly, "but I don't see no sense in taking chances. A war party of Arapahoes or Utes might go by and take a swipe at us."

Kirby had not heard any criticism of him, and he wondered why Thorn thought there would be some now. He glanced at the train captain, hearing a tone of uneasiness he had never noticed before. Thorn was the kind of man who gave the impression of being dead sure about everything. This, plus his record of always being right, inspired confidence in others and was largely responsible for his success as a train captain. For him to worry about criticism now seemed ridiculous.

Kirby shrugged, knowing it was not anything he could pursue. He watched the last wagon swing into place. Bill Jones stepped down from the seat as his sister Suzy rode up on her bay pony and said something to him.

Everyone in the party knew that Bill Jones was a proslavery man just as they knew Kirby was an abolitionist, but before the caravan left Linn County, Dave Thorn had ruled that anyone who started an argument

6

over the slavery question would be expelled from the train. The ruling had been a wise one. If it had not been made, the party would have broken up before it reached the Kaw.

"Each of us had his reasons for coming," Kirby said moodily. "I guess they'll all come out now."

"Don't push it, Kirby," Thorn said sharply.

Kirby grinned and nodded. They'd had a talk before they left Linn County. Thorn had said flatly that Kirby was a firebrand and he couldn't join the train unless he promised to lean over backwards to avoid trouble, so Kirby had promised.

"All right, Dave," Kirby said. "I'll keep my promise."

He started to turn his buckskin toward the creek, but pulled up when Thorn called, "Kirby, I'd like to talk to you after supper. Will you come to my wagon for a few minutes?"

Again Kirby had the feeling that Thorn was uneasy about something, then the thought struck him that the man was going to ask for help. This was so ridiculous that he dismissed the notion at once. Dave Thorn was the kind of man who gave help, not one who sought it, particularly from someone less than half his age.

"Sure, I'll be there," Kirby said.

This time Thorn let him ride down the bank to the shallow stream that meandered across a sandy bottom. He dismounted and loosened the cinch on his mount, the thought nagging him that perhaps Dave Thorn wasn't the strong man Kirby had pictured him. Possibly, now that he had arrived, the prospect of living in this so-called Jefferson Territory had unnerved him.

In reality there was little law and order out here. The governor and legislature of Jefferson Territory had no authority because the territory had not been recognized by Congress. The Pikes Peak country was in Kansas, but Kansas couldn't be bothered with its problems, and ignored it. Whatever law and order was here came from the towns and mining camps, existing on the local level because the people made it work. Even so, Denver was a violent town.

Kirby had never been out here before, but he knew this. Dave Thorn knew it too. Conditions would get worse with the Presidential election only weeks away and the prospect of civil war growing daily. Some of the people in the wagon train held no deep conviction about slavery, while others had been involved in robbery and burning and murder, for Linn County was cruelly torn by the fight between the Border Ruffians and the jay-hawkers.

"Bloody Kansas" was exactly that as far as Linn County was concerned. Probably most of the families that made up the wagon train were moving west to escape the trouble that still plagued eastern Kansas, but they might not be bettering themselves. This possibility could be what was nagging Dave Thorn.

The buckskin nuzzled Kirby. He patted the animal's neck as he said, "Bucky, you've got to get used to this thin air. We're going to be doing a lot of traveling."

Kirby started to turn, but stopped as Suzy Jones put her bay over the edge of the bank and reined up beside him. She was the wildest, sometimes he thought the craziest, girl he had ever met. She rode as well as any man in the wagon train, she acted as if she didn't know what it was to be afraid, and more than once on the Smoky Hill she had wandered too far from the wagons, and Thorn had sent Kirby after her.

She slid out of the saddle and let her horse drink. Cocking her head, she grinned at Kirby as she said, "You don't approve of me, do you, Mr. Grant? Well, maybe I don't approve of you. I think you're a stick-in-the-mud and I also think you need to be jolted up a little."

Holding the reins in her right hand, she took two steps toward him and hit him in the stomach with her left fist. She said, "Like that."

He said, "Oof" as air went out of his lungs. He hadn't expected it, but then he never knew what to expect from her. For a moment he glared at her, tempted to take her across his knee and spank her.

She was barely five feet tall, so short that she had to tip her head back to see his face. Her hair was bright red, and she possessed the temper that supposedly went with red hair. Kirby had experienced a few explosions of that temper, and now, looking down at her bright blue eyes and her full lips that were slightly parted, he knew exactly what she wanted, and decided to give it to her.

He swept her into his arms and kissed her. He supposed that she would fight him, pretending it was not what she wanted at all, but there was no pretense about her. Her arms encircled his neck; her kiss burned and shocked him with its intensity. The wildness was gone from her, and she was sweet and yielding in his embrace. When he finally let her go, he saw the fire that lingered in her eyes.

"Oh, honey," she said softly, "I've wanted you to do that for a long time. Why have you been so slow?"

"I was just waiting to get hit in the stomach," he said.

She giggled. "Sometimes a woman has to take strong measures to attract a man."

"You know what Bill would do if he saw me kiss you?" he demanded.

"What my brother Bill doesn't know won't hurt him," she said. "Anyhow, Bill wouldn't care. Politics has nothing to do with this."

He had known her for more than a year in Kansas, and they had been together a good deal the past thirty-five days; they had talked and fought and ridden together, and yet he had never realized how warm and exciting she was. He thought involuntarily, I'm twenty-three, more than old enough to take a wife and start a family and have a home. It's what I want, what any man wants. Kirby reined in his mind. Right now he couldn't let himself think about anything that would tie him down. He simply couldn't let a woman take the risks he would be taking.

Now, looking down at Suzy's expressive face, eager and expectant, he wondered if he could hold to his resolve.

Men were bringing their teams down the bank to water them. Al McCoy, who worked for Dave Thorn, drove Thorn's horse herd to the stream. Bill Jones, on up the creek about fifty yards, was watching Kirby and Suzy intently. Suddenly Kirby was angry.

"Are you trying to promote a fight between me and Bill?" he demanded.

"No, but it would be a good fight, wouldn't it?" she asked. "I think you could whip him."

He groaned. "I don't aim to try. Now stay away from me or we'll have some real trouble that won't do us any good."

"I'm not going to stay away from you," she said, "and I don't think you're afraid of trouble. Bill can believe what he wants to and you can believe—"

"Suzy, I may have to kill Bill or he may kill me," Kirby interrupted. "That's how important politics is and don't you forget it."

He wheeled away from her and started leading his buckskin up the bank. Suzy ran after him and caught his arm. "I'm going to see you tonight after everybody is asleep. I've got to talk to you."

He looked down at her and shook his head. "Have you gone daft? There have been dozens of times since we started that you could have talked to me alone, but no, you wait until we're only one day from the end of the trip and you're going to come in the middle of the night."

"That's right," she said. "When I wake you up, you come with me without making any fuss. We'll get far enough from camp so nobody can hear us."

"No you won't," he said. "That's all it would take for Bill to kill me."

He jerked free from her grip and went on up the bank. He off-saddled, staked his horse out, and picked up an armload of wood. He strode toward camp, thinking about the kiss and how she had thrown herself at him, and for the first time wished that he had a different

11

reason for coming to Jefferson Territory.

As far as he knew, the others in the wagon train were here to mine, to find new homes, to take advantage of any opportunities that might come to them, but Kirby Grant had a far different reason for coming. He was a member of a secret society in Kansas known as the Brotherhood of Free Soilers. He had taken an oath to obey his commanding officer and do anything in his power to bring Kansas into the Union as a free state. Now the same problem that faced the Free Soilers in Kansas also faced them in the Pikes Peak mining country. Sooner or later this area would be organized by Congress as a territory, and there were many in Denver, or so Kirby had heard, who would do and were doing all they could to make it a slave territory. But there was a Denver chapter of the Brotherhood, and Kirby had been sent to work with them. He did not know who belonged, or who the commanding officer was, but they knew he was coming, and he would be met, and only then would he know what he was expected to do. Whatever his assignment was, he thought, it was bound to be dangerous and lonesome. He couldn't even write to his folks while he was out here, because the Denver postmaster was known for his Southern sympathies.

His thoughts turned to Suzy again and he wondered what it was she wanted to talk about. She was wild and crazy and harum-scarum, but she was smart. She wouldn't take the risk unless whatever she had to say was important. She would come. He was as sure of that as he could be sure of anything about a woman as unpredictable as Suzy Jones.

T WO

KIRBY traveled light, hoping to return to Kansas in the spring, so he had made arrangements with his friend Duke Rome to haul his trunk and bedroll in Duke's wagon. Duke was two years older than Kirby, handsome, glib of speech, and skillful with the women. His parents had died of typhoid fever the year before, so there had been nothing to hold him in Linn County. When he'd heard that a wagon train was being made up to go to the Pikes Peak mines, he'd promptly sold his farm and joined the train.

He didn't know what he wanted to do, but he did know he wanted to get out of Kansas. Maybe he'd mine, but first he'd look things over. He told Kirby he had enough money to get through the first winter, so he'd take it easy in Denver, and when the weather warmed up in the spring, he'd start looking for something.

Kirby, who'd been his neighbor in Kansas and knew him well, thought that he'd be looking for something before spring. He was as improvident as a ten-year-old boy, and it was Kirby's guess that the sharpies in Denver would pluck him clean before the month was out.

Kirby built a fire and started supper. That had been the agreement. Duke would look after the wagon and team, and he'd haul Kirby's belongings. Kirby, in return, would take care of the fire and the cooking for both of them. They had split the cost of their supplies, and Kirby had been lucky in bringing in camp meat while they were on the road, both antelope and buffalo, so they had more than half of their supplies left. Kirby was glad it had worked out that way because the cost of food would be high in Denver.

Duke walked to the wagon in his leggy stride. He was the same height as Kirby, but not as heavy in the shoulders, so he appeared taller than he actually was. He dropped into the dry grass beside the fire as he said, "I hope you've got the grub ready. My tapeworm has been crawling up my backbone for the last hour."

"You're always hungry," Kirby said. "What are you going to do when you get to Denver—rent a cabin and cook for yourself?"

"Hell, no. I ain't no cook. I'd starve to death before Christmas." Duke paused, glancing across the wagon circle to the Riley wagon, then he said slowly, "Kirby, what do you think of Laurabelle?"

Kirby turned the bacon, not saying anything for a time. He liked Laurie Riley and felt sorry for her. She was eighteen but immature for her age, a slender girl who was not as fragile as she appeared. She had been a hard worker when she'd been home. Still, she needed a couple more years before she could cope with the rough life she would have to face out here. At times she seemed almost childlike, and Kirby had found himself worrying about her more than anyone else in the wagon train.

Laurabelle's father, Sam Riley, had tried to farm a mile or so from the Grant place in Kansas, but in spite of his good intentions, he never seemed to get anything done. He professed to be an abolitionist and had helped move a few runaway slaves to the next station on the underground railroad, but Kirby's father had never really trusted the man, partly because he talked too much. Now he was out here in the mining country with his daughter. He had no money, his horses were the poorest in the caravan, and he'd had more trouble keeping up than any of the others. As Dave Thorn had said, his wagon was held together by wire and spit.

"Well?" Duke prompted. "You ain't answering my question. You've known Laurabelle longer'n I have."

"Yea, I guess," Kirby said. "They've been our neighbors ever since we moved to Linn County, so I've kind of watched her grow up. She's a nice girl, Duke, but that's the trouble. She is a girl. She just hasn't quite managed to grow into a woman."

Duke shrugged. "She's a dandy cook. I was in their cabin a few times and she always had everything up to snuff. As far as I'm concerned, that makes her a woman."

"Well, then," Kirby said, "maybe she's just what you want, but don't forget her pa. He's mostly talk and not much on doing. Always full of excuses and complaining about his bad luck."

"He ain't much for a fact," Duke said, "but maybe he'll be glad to get Laurabelle off his hands. I figure on asking her to marry me, tonight if I can get her by herself. They say Colorado winters are mighty cold, so maybe she'd keep me warm."

Kirby was afraid this was in Duke's mind. Duke had spent most of the evenings with Laurie since they'd left Linn County, and judging from the way the girl looked at him, Kirby had a feeling she'd say yes the instant he asked her to marry him.

The marriage wasn't right for her, Kirby thought. She needed a strong man who would love and cherish her. With enough time and love, she would make a good wife, but Duke loved Duke first of all, and he was not a patient man. But at that, Laurie might be better off married to Duke than if she stayed with her father.

"Well, you just ain't real happy about me'n Laurabelle, seems like," Duke grumbled.

"No, I'm not," Kirby said. "I figure you're being shortsighted. I know Sam pretty well. He'll be mooching off you the first week and you won't like it."

"I sure as hell won't," Duke admitted amiably. "If he comes around my cabin looking for a handout, I'll kick his butt into Cherry Creek."

"And you'll make Laurie unhappy," Kirby said.

Duke spread his hands as if that was his affair. "I'm marrying Laurabelle, not Sam," he said. "The sooner they find that out, the better."

Kirby pulled the frying pan off the fire, thinking the solution was not that easy, not if a man truly loved the girl he was marrying. But Duke was the kind who could shed responsibility with a shrug of his shoulders. If he was marrying Laurie for no better reason than to keep him warm at night, he certainly would not be concerned about Sam Riley.

Kirby had put up with his partner's selfishness because he knew they would be separated as soon as they reached Denver. Perhaps they would never see each other again. The country was big, life was violent and death was often sudden. The chances were that one or both would not live through the winter. But marrying Laurie was another matter. She was a sweet and innocent girl who had been shortchanged by life, and she deserved a better destiny than being married to Duke Rome. No, she wouldn't be better off married than if she stayed with her father.

He reached for the coffeepot and filled his tin cup, and then, because he couldn't stand it any longer, he burst out, "Don't marry her, Duke."

"Why not?" Duke demanded.

"I told you she was still a girl."

"Maybe you think I ain't good enough for her."

"I didn't say that."

Duke flicked his tin cup toward the fire, the coffee that was in the cup making a sizzling sound as it struck a burning cottonwood limb. "I'm guessing it's what you meant. Maybe you're jealous. Maybe you was figuring on marrying her yourself."

At least they had reached Cherry Creek before they quarreled, Kirby thought. He rose from where he had been hunkering beside the fire and sipped his coffee for a time. Finally he said, "No, Duke, I'm not figuring on marrying Laurie."

"It's a good thing," Duke said hotly. "The way you and Suzy was lallygagging down by the creek this evening, I'd say you didn't have no business thinking 'bout Laurabelle. You better get Suzy out in the brush tonight and take care of her."

That was like Duke, Kirby thought; it was the way his mind ran. He finished the coffee, anger growing in him. "Now that you raise the point, I might as well tell you I *don't* think you're good enough for Laurie. I don't think you're ready to settle down with a wife and a batch of babies."

"By God, I ain't having no batch of babies," Duke said with cold fury. "And who the hell are you to tell me what I'm ready for and what I ain't? Get your bedroll and trunk out of my wagon." He started to walk away, then wheeled back. "Get 'em out while I'm gone."

He strode away. Kirby, staring at his slim, straight-backed figure, thought it was a good thing they hadn't quarreled somewhere back on the Smoky Hill. He'd have had a hard time carrying his bedroll and trunk on his buckskin.

THREE

T HE day had been a warm one, but now that they were so close to the mountains, the air took on a penetrating chill as soon as the sun went down. Kirby carried his bedroll and trunk to the Thorn wagon, thinking he'd better dig out his coat. He had a hunch the temperature would drop below freezing by morning, and from what he'd heard about the quick weather changes in this country, he might wake up to find snow on the ground.

Dave Thorn was smoking his pipe beside his fire as Kirby came up. His wife Liz had just finished cleaning up after supper, but the coffeepot was still in the coals at the edge of the fire. She was younger than Thorn by at least five years, Kirby guessed. Although her hair was completely white, she retained a youthful face and figure.

The pressing heat, the violent storms, the dust that worked into a person's eyes and nose and ears, the mosquitoes that at times seemed unbearable, the fatigue that came from bone-jarring hours spent in the wagon seat: these were the hardships that had made other women in the train nervous and irritable, but as far as Kirby had been able to tell they hadn't even made Liz Thorn grumpy. She was, by Kirby's standards, a truly wonderful woman.

As Kirby dropped his bedroll and sat down on his trunk, Mrs. Thorn asked, "Have a cup of coffee?"

"No thanks," he said. "I just finished." He turned to Thorn. "Have you got room for my bedroll and trunk?"

"Sure, but what's wrong with Rome's wagon?" Thorn asked.

"We had a little difficulty." Kirby told him what had happened, adding, "I guess I have a talent for poking my nose into other folks' business, but the more I thought about it, the madder I got. If Duke had said he loved Laurie, I'd have kept my mouth shut, but he never said it. We neighbored with the Rileys back home. I guess Ma felt obligated to look after Laurie, her not having a mother. Maybe that's why I'm concerned about her now."

"It's a crying shame," Mrs. Thorn said indignantly. "I don't know either one as well as you do, Kirby, but I can see what you mean about Laurie. She just don't know enough to get married yet, not to a man like Duke Rome anyhow."

"Sure," Thorn said, "but it ain't your business no more than it's Kirby's. I ain't being critical, son, so don't misunderstand me. A man has to do what he's driven to do by something inside him. All I'm saying is that if two grown people decide to do something, you can't keep 'em from doing it even if you're sure it's wrong."

Mrs. Thorn sniffed. "Well, a body has to try, David. She's young and innocent, and she don't have no older woman to tell her about things. All she's got is that terrible loud-mouthed father."

"No, Liz," Thorn said firmly. "A body doesn't have to try. You're putting yourself in God's shoes, but you don't have His wisdom. Rome might make her a good husband. We don't know for sure. You don't know what will happen to her if she stays with her father, either. Suppose you talk her into turning Rome down and she goes on into Denver with Sam Riley and he gets killed? What's going to happen to her?"

Mrs. Thorn sighed. "I suppose you're right, David. You always are." She turned to Kirby. "What are you going to do when you get to Denver?"

He was startled by her direct question. He couldn't give her an honest answer, and he was afraid she was too discerning to be fooled by one that wasn't honest. He hesitated, then he said, "I guess I'll have to look around, Liz."

"We want you to live with us," she said. "I know we can't take the place of your parents—"

"Hod dang it, woman," Thorn said angrily. "That was what I was going to talk to Kirby about. Why don't you go visit with somebody for half an hour?" He jerked his head toward the Jones wagon. "Looks like Suzy ain't busy."

Liz smiled, unperturbed by his outburst. "All right, David. Now I was saying, Kirby, that we don't have no children, but I guess that if I had a son, I'd want him to be like you. We're alone out here in a wild country of strangers, so we'd like it if you called our place your home as long as you want to."

Without a glance at her husband, she gathered her skirt in one hand and walked rapidly toward the Jones wagon. Thorn scowled at Kirby as he took his pipe out of his mouth. "Damn sentimental woman. She'll adopt you if you let her." He knocked his pipe out against his heel and suddenly grinned. "Not that I'd care. It's just that I had another line of attack in mind."

Kirby took his pipe from his pocket and filled it, surprised because he had never found either Thorn or his wife devious people, but he was convinced that they were being devious now and this scene had been prearranged.

"All right," he said. "Go ahead and attack."

Thorn remained silent for a time. His pipe had gone out. He leaned forward and, picking up a burning cottonwood twig, lighted the tobacco. Twilight had thinned until it was almost dark, and now the women were calling their children in from the creek where they had been playing. Several young people including Laurie and Duke Rome had gathered around one of the fires and were singing "Sweet Betsy from Pike" and "Yellow Rose of Texas." Suddenly the group broke up, Duke taking Laurabelle's hand and leading her between two of the wagons into the thickening dusk.

"I guess I'm a little scared, Kirby," Thorn said finally.

"Maybe Denver won't turn out to be as tough a town as I expect to find, but we know there is a bunch of organized toughs called the Bummers. Then there's the Vigilantes, that they call the Stranglers. I'm not scared of a fight—I've been in plenty of them—but I am scared of the kind of atmosphere we're going to find here. I wish I hadn't brought Liz along."

So this was what had been bothering Thorn. Kirby fired his pipe, then took it out of his mouth. He said, "None of them will bother a good woman, Dave."

"Maybe not," Thorn said, "but it's still enough to worry a man. I was thinking that along with the lawlessness that's already here, there's bound to be more trouble if Lincoln is elected. We're a long ways from slave territory, but people have brought their beliefs with them. Take Sam Riley, who talks so much. He'll express himself to the wrong man and he'll get shot. That's one reason I didn't want Liz to bother Laurabelle one way or the other. She may need Rome if she don't have a father."

"She'll need somebody," Kirby agreed.

"Well, what I'm getting around to saying is that folks know your feelings," Thorn said, "You've sure got a right to think what you want to, but I ain't sure you've got a right to say what you want to in Denver. It'd be like dropping a lighted match into a barrel of powder."

Kirby tamped the tobacco down into the bowl of his pipe, not sure what Thorn was driving at. The train captain had never been a man to express himself freely on controversial subjects, and even as well as Kirby knew him, there were some doubts in his mind about Thorn's attitude toward slavery. He had said he believed the Union must be held together and he couldn't vote for Breckinridge. He was probably a Douglas man, but Kirby wasn't even sure of that.

"I don't know what you're getting at," Kirby said finally, "but I don't aim to go up and down the street yelling at everybody and telling them what I think."

"Good." Thorn smiled briefly. "I didn't figure you would. I'd like for you to work for me, Kirby, and I want to stay out of trouble. I don't know exactly what your reasons are for coming out here, so I thought I'd better quiz you a little bit."

"You hadn't said anything about working for you before." Kirby shook his head. "I don't know about it, Dave. I didn't plan on taking a job till I'd looked around a little."

"Maybe I should have mentioned it sooner," Thorn said. "You see, the closer I got to Denver, the more uneasy I felt. I have some gold in my wagon, but most of my money is tied up in my horses. I'd be in a hell of a fix if they were stolen and I had to start over. McCoy's a good man, but he's not the fighter you are. How about it?"

Kirby glanced briefly at Thorn and saw the desperate hope in the man's face. The thought came to him that Dave Thorn was a frightened man hiding behind the façade of self-assurance and dignity he showed others. Al McCoy was a hired man, no more and no less, and Thorn knew he could not be counted on when the blue chip was down, just as he knew Kirby Grant could.

For a moment Kirby was filled with resentment when

he remembered Liz's talk about making their place his home. Now Dave Thorn was trying to hire loyalty. But he might be wrong. Liz could have meant what she said and maybe Thorn was not as frightened as Kirby was thinking. He could help Thorn out at least till the Brotherhood got in touch with him.

"All right," Kirby said finally. "For a while anyway. I'll help you get settled."

"Good," Thorn said. "Tomorrow I'm going to stop a few miles out of Denver and hold the wagon and horses there while I go into town. I'll try to buy a livery stable if I can. If not, I'll build one. Liz and McCoy will stay with you and the horses."

Thorn rose as if everything was arranged. Liz returned and stopped for a moment at the fire. She said, "Suzy is a nice girl. I hope she finds a husband out here. A good one, I mean. With all the single men running around in a new country like this, I'm sure she can find somebody, but she'll be choosy and she ought to be."

"Leave your trunk right there, Kirby," Thorn said. "We'll find a place in the wagon tomorrow."

He disappeared into the darkness. Liz asked, "Are you going to work for us?"

"I said I would for a while," he answered.

He had a disturbing feeling she was disappointed by his answer. She said quickly, "That's fine, Kirby. Just fine," and he wondered if he was imagining her reaction.

She turned toward the wagon and disappeared inside. Kirby remained beside the fire until he finished his pipe. Suddenly he realized that he was uneasy and he wasn't sure why. Perhaps he had caught it from Thorn.

He saw Laurie and Duke Rome come out of the darkness and pause for a moment beside the Riley fire, Rome acting very possessive, then he crossed the inside of the circle to his wagon. Kirby knew, then. He was worried about Laurie more than he had any right to be. She was like a stray kitten that no one wanted to claim. In the end maybe he'd be the one who would have to look out for her.

FOUR

KIRBY lay awake a long time. He wasn't sure why he couldn't sleep unless it was the fact that they were only a day's journey from Denver, but he would not be seeing it tomorrow when most of the wagon train pulled into town. He'd be with Mrs. Thorn and McCoy and the horses somewhere along Cherry Creek. In a way Dave Thorn had trapped him and he'd been sucker enough to stay trapped.

He should have told Thorn he was going on with the rest, and Thorn could put his horses in the Elephant Corral in Denver if he was afraid they'd be stolen. But Thorn had been cute. He hadn't really given Kirby a chance to say anything of the kind. He waited until Kirby had said he'd work for him and then he'd given his order and walked off.

Well, it didn't make any real difference, he told himself. Denver wouldn't go away. Chances were it wasn't much to see. It would be like any frontier town, dusty and without shade and made up of tents and log cabins. Then, because he couldn't sleep, he began thinking about the trip from Linn County to Cherry Creek.

There had been an argument before they'd started about whether they would swing north and follow the Overland Trail up Platte River or take the Smoky Hill which was the shortest trail to the mines by at least two hundred miles. The Leavenworth people claimed it was only six hundred ten miles from their town on the Kansas-Missouri line to Denver. Furthermore, the Smoky Hill did not have the stretches of sand that slowed wagons on the Overland.

Everyone agreed that the Smoky Hill was shorter than either the Overland to the north or the Santa Fe Trail to the south. Dave Thorn argued that this was important. Starting so late in the season, he said, they had to consider distance above everything else. Others reminded him of the horror stories that had been brought back by gold seekers who had followed the Smoky Hill, stories of men starving to death or dying of thirst or exhaustion, of murder on the trail and even of cannibalism.

After he had listened to these tales, and had heard William N. Byers's *Rocky Mountain News* quoted—Byers had called it the "Smoky Hell route"—Thorn said simply, "I'll get you through."

He'd had his way, and he had not had the slightest doubt about himself then, Kirby thought; he had shown no trace of uneasiness.

He'd kept his word, Kirby reflected. He had brought them through. It had not been an easy trip, but then it wouldn't have been an easy trip by way of the Overland or the Santa Fe. They would have taken at least ten more days, ten very disagreeable days if an early storm had hit them.

Kirby remembered the time when someone at a place called First View had yelled, "There's Pikes Peak." They had all seen it then, no more than a tiny cloud on the horizon, and even though they knew it was a long way off, they had the comforting knowledge that the Rockies were within sight.

After that the mountains had appeared and disappeared and appeared again as they crossed the rolling prairie. Later, from the Sandy-Bijou Divide, Pikes Peak had seemed very near. Then they had seen a long stretch of the still distant range as far north as Long's Peak, some of the taller mountains showing a dusting of snow from an early storm.

Kirby yawned sleepily, thinking it was not a trip he or anyone else in the party would soon forget. They had seen mining tools, cookstoves, furniture, and even a plow that had been thrown away by travelers who had gone before them. Skeletons of mules and horses and oxen lay beside the road, and they had seen ravens and wolves feeding on carcasses of animals that had died recently.

Yes, it was a trip he would remember. Perhaps if he had plenty of time, he would take the Overland when he returned to Linn County next spring or summer. Or he might stay out here, although he had no intention of prospecting for gold. The real future of the mining country was probably many years ahead, when transportation was better and there was enough local capital to buy machinery to work the ore. Meanwhile, if some of the wild talk coming out of the South was to be taken seriously, war was not far away. If it came, his place would be back home.

For a moment he lay staring at the sky, thinking how distance in this thin, clear air fooled a man. Out here the stars seemed much closer than they were in Kansas, so close that if he had a longer arm, he could reach up and touch them. The thought amused him and he laughed softly as he fell asleep.

He woke with someone bending over him. It was still night. For a moment he was groggy, then he became aware that a soft hand lay over his mouth, and a woman was saying, "Wake up, darling. I told you I'd see you tonight."

Suzy! He was fully awake and remembering. She'd hit him in the stomach and he'd kissed her and she'd said that sometimes a woman had to take strong measures to attract a man. He'd told her to let him alone, but here she was in the middle of the night just as she had said she'd be.

He grabbed her hand and jerked it away from his mouth. He said, "You get out of here. I told you—"

Her hand was over his mouth again. "Shhh," she said. "Are you trying to wake the whole camp?"

"No." This time he whispered, wondering if he had spoken loudly enough to wake anybody. That was the last thing he wanted. "Will you please let me alone?"

"Not until you get up and come far enough away so we can talk."

"I won't do it. I told you—"

"I know what you told me," she said, "but you love me, don't you?"

"I don't love you. Just because I kissed you—"

"We can't discuss it here, so get up and come with me. Maybe you'll change your mind after you kiss me again."

He groaned. "All I want is for you—"

"You'd better quit arguing or I'll scream and wake up the whole camp."

"You wouldn't do—"

"Oh, yes I would. I'd even tear my dress and say you did it. They'd hang you. I'd hate to see the man I love hung, so you'd better come quietly."

"My God, I believe you're crazy enough to do it."

"Sure I am, honey," she said. "Come on."

He threw back the blanket and picked up the coat he had taken out of his trunk before he went to bed. She took his hand and led him away from the wagons. He looked down at her in the starlight, completely confused.

She had been wild and irresponsible many times on the trail, but this was crazy. No decent woman would throw herself at a man like this, and Suzy Jones was a decent woman. This was something he could not doubt. It was just that she had thought of some kind of a prank. Her brother Bill was a serious-minded man, but Suzy had always been a practical joker.

"This is far enough," she said. "We can talk if we keep our voices down."

She dropped into the dry grass beside the bank of Cherry Creek. She was still holding his hand and now she pulled him down beside her. He asked, "Why didn't you go to Duke's wagon to get me?"

"Liz told me what happened," Suzy answered. "She said you were going to throw your stuff into their

29

wagon." She hesitated, then she said, "I feel sorry for Laurie, but I don't know what either one of us can do for her." She paused again, and said slowly as if afraid she would offend Kirby, "I'm glad Liz told me where you were. I'd be afraid to wake Duke Rome up the way I did you, and I would never be out here alone with him in the dark."

"Why?"

"It's just a feeling I have about him. Liz feels the same way. It's kind of queer, too. I don't feel that way about many men."

"You don't seem to be afraid of me."

For a moment she had been deadly serious, but now she laughed softly. "No, you're a man of honor. I'm cold. Will you be honorable enough to do something about that."

He draped his coat around her shoulders. "How's that?"

"Oh, that's fine for keeping me warm," she said, "but the trouble is my back hurts. It needs support, like a good strong arm to lean against."

He groaned. "You tempt me," he said.

He put his arm around her and she snuggled against him. "I tempt you to what?" she asked.

"To slit your throat," he said. "Or break your neck. Or kiss you."

"I'll accept the last temptation," she said, and tipped her head back.

He kissed her, and when she drew away a moment later, she said, "I know you'll make a good husband, Kirby. When are we getting married?"

"I never said I was going to marry you," he said. "I don't have honorable intentions and you might as well know it. Not unless Bill wakes up and decides this occasion calls for a shotgun."

"He might at that," she said, serious again. "My brother Bill is a man of strict morals, but people are not always what they seem to be."

"What do you mean by that?"

"It's what I wanted to talk to you about," she said. "Bill wanted to talk to you, too, but the right opportunity to talk without being spied on never came along, so I told him I'd do it." She paused, then asked, "Bill says we'll be in Denver late tomorrow afternoon. What are you going to do?"

Her mercurial moods puzzled him. She was teasing him one moment, and gravely serious the next. He thought about it, but he could not think of any logical reason for the changes. Maybe the reason, whatever it was, simply wasn't logical.

"I'm not going into Denver," he said. "I told Dave I'd work for him for a while."

"Kirby, you're not going to," she cried.

"I said for a while. He asked me to."

"You've got to go into Denver tomorrow, Kirby. You've got to."

"It'll still be there when I have time to go. Dave wants to look things over and buy a stable if he can. I'm staying with the wagon and horses somewhere along the creek on this side of Denver. McCoy and Liz will be with me."

She stiffened, then suddenly she jerked out of his

embrace and jumped up. She said hotly, "They'll kill you."

He rose, more confused than ever and not having the slightest idea who the "they" were. She was furious with him. He knew all he wanted to about her temper, and usually it took quite a bit to set it off, but this time he couldn't think of anything he had done or said to trigger it.

"You idiot!" she cried passionately. "You stupid idiot. They'll kill you if—"

He wheeled away from her and strode back to the wagon. Let her have her tantrum by herself, he thought. He wanted no part of it. Then a man loomed out of the darkness ahead of him, and he heard Bill Jones bellow, "I'm going to beat you to death, Grant. No goddamned abolitionist is gonna take my sister out into the brush."

Kirby stopped, telling himself that Suzy and her brother were out of their minds, then Jones was on him, his fists swinging out ponderously, and he had the terrifying feeling that he was fighting for his life, that Bill Jones would kill him if he could.

FIVE

KIRBY retreated before Jones's attack. He had no reason to fight the man and he didn't want to, but he couldn't stand still and get his head knocked off, either. Crazy or not, Jones was powerfully built and could hurt him, so Kirby continued to move back. He kept just out of Jones's reach, circling warily and hoping that Suzy would appear and tell her wild man of a brother that nothing had happened to make him act this way.

Men, awakened by the commotion, had hastily pulled on their pants and were rushing toward the fighters. Dave Thorn was there, holding his lantern high, and then Duke Rome made his appearance, yelling derisively, "Why don't you stand still and fight, Grant?"

Someone else—it sounded like Sam Riley, Laurie's father—shouted, "He's outrunning you, Bill, and going backwards to boot."

Then Duke Rome again, "Run faster, Bill. You can catch him."

Jones crowded Kirby, throwing another ponderous punch. Kirby had plenty of time to duck, for he had seen it coming even in the murky light from the lanterns that the men were carrying. It was plain by now that Suzy wasn't coming to stop the fight, and it also seemed plain that if Bill Jones ever connected with one of his round-house blows, Kirby would be knocked silly. It was time to stop it before he got hurt.

Kirby moved forward one step, his right coming through in a sledging blow. The counterattack was swift and unexpected, and Jones, a little off balance as a result of missing the punch he had thrown, was wide open. Kirby's fist caught him on the side of the face, the sound of the blow a kind of thudding *thwack*.

Jones sprawled on his back, his arms flung out on the grass. Kirby jumped on top of him and hit him on one side of the face and then the other. They rolled over, Jones hugging him with both arms as he said, "You need to make it look good, but not this good."

They rolled over again, Kirby having no more idea

what Jones was talking about than he'd had of several of the things Suzy had said. Then Liz Thorn, running toward them, screamed, "Pull 'em apart, Dave. They've got nothing to fight over. Suzy's asleep in her wagon."

Thorn and some of the others caught Kirby's arms and lifted him to his feet as two more men grabbed Jones's shoulders and hoisted him to an upright position. He slumped in their grip, too groggy to stand by himself. Blood trickled down his upper lip from his nose. He swiped a sleeve across his mouth, muttering, "What'd you say, Liz?"

"I heard what you said when you jumped Kirby," Mrs. Thorn snapped. "I must say you're mighty anxious to fight or else you just can't see straight. Suzy is in her bed in the wagon. She'd been asleep until you started this row. Now you just apologize and go on back to your own bed."

Jones swiped at the blood again. "I reckon I don't know my own sister in the dark. I'm sorry I jumped you, Kirby." He broke through the circle of men and reeled toward his wagon. His rubbery knees failed to hold him and he fell. He got up and went on.

Kirby stared after him, thinking there had been no serious trouble in the wagon train from the morning they'd left Linn County till now, when they were only fifteen miles from Denver. First Suzy had gone into a rage and told him somebody would kill him, and then Bill Jones had jumped him.

Did Suzy mean Bill would kill him for taking care of Dave Thorn's horses, that Bill was going to try to steal them? No, she couldn't have meant that. Jones wasn't a horse thief, whatever else he might be. Then he'd said something about not making it look that good. Well, the Jones family must have a streak of insanity running through it.

All the men except Duke Rome had returned to their beds now that the excitement was over. Rome stood motionless, barring Kirby's path. He was breathing as if he had just come in from a hard run.

"Get out of my way, Duke," Kirby said harshly. "I heard you yelling for me to stand and fight and for Bill to run faster. If you want to pick it up where Bill dropped it, go ahead."

"You had some woman out in the brush, didn't you?" Duke demanded hoarsely. "Bill saw you with a woman and mistook her for Suzy because he seen you lallygagging with her on the creek."

Kirby clenched his fists at his sides, fighting an impulse to knock Duke down. He said, "I told you to get out of my way."

"I've got something to tell you first," Duke said. "I asked Laurie to marry me. You knowed I was going to, and you was sore about it and said I wasn't good enough for Laurie. I figure she was the one you was with tonight. If I knowed for sure, I'd kill you right now."

"You son of a bitch." Kirby said. "You sure trust her, don't you?"

"I don't trust you," Duke flung at him. "How about it? Was she the one?"

"No."

"You're a goddamned liar. I—"

Kirby let his temper go then. He drove a fist into

Duke's stomach that sent air whistling out of his lungs. As Duke bent forward trying to breathe, one hand clutching his middle, Kirby hit him on the jaw and knocked him down.

Kirby walked past him and went on to the Thorn wagon as Dave Thorn came toward him holding his lantern. He asked, "More trouble?"

"Not much," Kirby said. "It's over."

Thorn returned to his bed and blew out his lantern. Kirby lay down and pulled the blanket over him. He wondered if the things that had happened in the last hour could be a nightmare. He'd had nightmares that made him feel this way, vivid experiences that had no logic to them. No, these things had actually happened, logic or not.

Wide-eyed, he stared at the sky. He refused to think about Suzy and her brother—there wasn't any use trying to figure them out; but he could understand Duke Rome, and he had a nagging thought that in spite of anything he could do, sooner or later one of them would kill the other.

He had known about Duke when they were neighbors, that the man was spoiled and weak, utterly selfish, and without conscience in dealing with women. But they'd got along, had even been friends in a way. At least Duke's antics had not bothered Kirby before, perhaps because he had never felt responsible for any of the women with whom Duke had had his affairs.

Laurie was different. She wasn't a woman. If she were, Kirby would have stayed out of it. Perhaps he would have stayed out of it anyway if Duke hadn't asked him what he thought of Laurie. No, in the end he would have made it his business because he felt a responsibility toward the girl.

He wasn't really sure why he felt that responsibility, or why his feelings for Suzy were so different. Maybe the difference was in the two, for Laurie was a trusting child, but Suzy was a woman who loved to play with fire and who could control it. She had a wonderful talent for taking care of herself wherever she was, and Laurie didn't. He'd find a chance tomorrow to talk to Laurie, he told himself. She simply couldn't marry Duke Rome.

He was still awake when dawn began to color the sky above the hills to the east, and the camp came awake. He was dead tired when he got up and trudged through the dry grass that crackled stiffly under his boots. He went into the brush along the bank, nodding at Dave Thorn who was coming back toward the wagon.

After he had gone by, Thorn said, "Kirby."

He turned and waited while Thorn walked back to stand beside him. He said in a low tone, "You'd better watch Duke. He'll shoot you in the back if he gets a chance."

"I figure he will," Kirby agreed. "It's a funny thing, Dave. You know a man for years, then all of a sudden you find out you don't know him at all. I didn't know Duke till last night."

"Now you do," Thorn said, and went on.

When Kirby knelt at the edge of the creek to wash his face, he discovered a thin layer of ice on the still water along the edge. When he rose and glanced at the dark clouds which were moving in from the mountains to the west, he thought they had arrived barely in time, that an early snowstorm was on the way.

He returned to the wagon, carrying an armload of wood. He squatted beside the fire as Mrs. Thorn cooked breakfast of bacon, flapjacks and coffee. Later, when Thorn went after the horses, Kirby said, "Liz, I'm going to talk to Laurie today and tell her not to marry Duke. Am I wrong?"

"You're asking for more trouble," she said. "Goodness knows you had enough last night, but I guess you're a man who can handle a lot of it."

"I asked you if I was wrong."

She studied him a moment, a hand coming up to brush back a lock of hair. She said thoughtfully, "Dave would say you were, but you know what he thinks. You heard him last night. He'd still say you're playing God."

"He knows Duke," Kirby said, "but he doesn't know Laurie. I've got to try."

"Do you love her?"

"Love her?" he asked. "That's a crazy question, Liz."

She shook her head. "No, it's a good question, Kirby. Do you?"

He thought about it a moment. If his purpose in coming out here was not what it was—if Suzy had been decently courteous and hadn't called him a stupid idiot—if her brother hadn't forced a fight, he might shock Liz and say he loved Suzy.

He grinned at Liz, thinking it would be funny if she knew what he was thinking. Maybe he was as stupid an idiot as Suzy accused him of being. In spite of everything that had happened, and in spite of all the reasons that he had kept in his mind so he would be cool about the whole business, he had fallen in love with Suzy Jones—red hair, temper, practical jokes, and all. Life with her would be a trial, but it would be an adventure, too. He couldn't tell her now, though. Maybe he could never tell her.

"No, Liz," he said. "I'm not in love with Laurie. It's just that she needs me."

"Yes, I think she does," Liz said, "but you'd better be careful. I doubt that Suzy would understand."

She began packing the pots and pans into a box. Kirby lifted his trunk into the wagon and tossed his bedroll on top of it. He told himself glumly that he felt sorry for Dave Thorn. It would be tough living with a woman who could read a man's mind the way Liz could.

SIX

THE sun was barely showing above the hills to the east when the wagon train uncurled from its circle and started the last day's journey. Now Kirby was really sorry he would not be with the train when it reached Denver. He still resented the way Dave Thorn had trapped him, too, but he'd made an agreement, and he had no valid grounds for breaking it.

Kirby rode in front beside Thorn. Liz drove their wagon, and Al McCoy was moving the horse herd upstream somewhere between the train and Cherry Creek. Kirby glanced at Thorn now and then, wondering what the man was thinking, but he couldn't read the expression on the bearded face. Dave Thorn stared straight ahead, the corners of his mouth working as they did when he buried himself in the private world of his thoughts.

Kirby shrugged and turned up the collar of his coat. One thing was certain: he was not a mind reader. Still, he couldn't let go of the fact that not once during the long journey along the Smoky Hill had he felt there was anything mysterious about Dave Thorn, but as soon as they reached Cherry Creek, Thorn seemed to have become a different man.

Kirby glanced westward, but the great peaks of the Rockies were hidden by swirling black clouds. The chances were good that there would be snow on the ground beside the wagon in the morning. Then his thoughts turned to Laurabelle Riley and he wondered what would happen to her. If she stayed with her father, she would probably have to live in their wagon all winter, but what would happen if she married Duke Rome?

She couldn't, he told himself. She just couldn't. He had told Liz he was going to talk to Laurie, then he'd decided not to. Dave Thorn was right and he shouldn't try playing God. He had no way of knowing how much she would mature this winter, and he realized there was a possibility she would be better off with Rome than with her father.

Now he changed his mind again. The more he thought about it, the more he was convinced that anything she did would be better than marrying Duke Rome. He was going to tell her what he thought even at the risk of making her angry. If she went ahead and married Rome anyhow, she would at least have been warned, and Kirby would have the comfort of knowing he had done all he could for her.

"I'm going back to see Laurie," Kirby said.

Thorn nodded, his mind apparently fixed on something far ahead. Kirby swung his horse around, nodded at Liz, and galloped back along the wagon train, convinced that Thorn had not even heard him. He raised a hand to Suzy as he passed the Jones wagon, and a moment later reached Duke Rome's outfit. He glanced at Rome, who ignored him. Kirby smiled and rode on. The feeling, he told himself, was mutual.

The Riley wagon was the last in the train. Kirby turned his buckskin and reined in beside it. He touched the brim of his hat and said, "Howdy."

Laurie said, "Good morning." She glanced at him and lowered her head in the scared way she had. She acted as if she were frightened of everyone and everything, Kirby thought, and fear had a way of snowballing in a person. It might make her turn to Rome because she thought he loved her and so would give her a security she'd never had with her father.

Sam Riley was chewing steadily on a huge quid of tobacco. Now he leaned over the wheel and spat a brown ribbon into the dust beside the road. He wiped a hairy hand across his mouth, leaving a brown stain on his lips.

"Well, Grant, we're just about there," Riley said. "Reckon we'll roll into town by the middle of the afternoon."

"That's about right," Kirby said.

Riley had an obnoxious way of talking as if he considered himself an oracle. Kirby told himself that a man as completely worthless as Sam Riley had to fool himself into thinking he was important or he wouldn't be able to face another day of living when he woke up each morning. Like most men of his kind, he blamed his poverty on bad luck. Kirby had never known him to blame himself.

Laurie must hate her father, Kirby thought. Perhaps she even hated herself for staying with him after her mother had died six years ago. He had not made a decent living as long as Kirby had known them, and he had often wondered why Laurie stayed on. She hadn't quite starved, and maybe she thought she would if she tried to make her own living.

"Reckon you heard that Laurabelle and young Rome are gonna get hitched," Riley said. "She's lucky to nab a man like him with enough money to get a start out here. I'm lucky, too. I won't have to worry about her no more. Duke'll look out for her." He nodded toward the mountains. "I dunno how much gold is up there, but I sure aim to get mine before it's all gone."

He wouldn't make a strike, Kirby thought. He'd walk right over a rich deposit of gold, and some other man coming behind him would see it and stake out a claim and make a fortune. Riley would tell about it the rest of his life and blame his bad luck for his failure.

Kirby didn't say anything. Neither did Laurie, who still sat beside her father, her gaze on her lap. She shivered and slipped her hands into the ends of her coat sleeves.

"We'll find a good camping place along the river just out of town," Riley said, "and then we'll see if we can wangle a nice wedding dress." He glanced at Kirby as if

42

seeking approval. "Her ma was a mighty purty woman when we got married. Lately Laurabelle does seem to favor her a lot."

Kirby wanted to tell Riley that if he'd been any kind of a man and had taken care of his wife, she'd be alive and still be a mighty pretty woman. But there was not use telling Sam Riley anything. Kirby couldn't stand any more of the man's know-it-all conversation; he said hastily, "Why don't you get down and walk a piece, Laurie? It'll warm you up."

She gave him a grateful glance. She said, "I'd like to. Papa, let me get down."

He pulled the team to a stop. "You keep up," he said. "I don't want to have to wait for you."

"Yes, Papa," she said, and stepped to the ground.

Kirby dismounted and walked beside her. They slowed their pace until the wagon was far enough ahead so Riley could not hear what they said.

"Maybe we shouldn't do this," Laurie said. "I'm not even sure I ought to be talking to you. Duke would be awful mad. I'm going to marry him, Kirby."

For the first time she turned her head to look at him and he saw worry clearly stamped upon her delicate features. Well, at least she was not jumping into this marriage without giving it serious thought.

"Are you worried about yourself or me?" Kirby asked, smiling.

"You," Laurie said quickly. "He's always nice to me, but I know you had a fight last night. I don't want to be the cause of another one."

"I handled him last night and I can handle him again,"

Kirby said. "What you should be doing is worrying about yourself. That's why I'm here. It's none of my business and you've got a right to tell me so, but we were neighbors and Ma was real fond of you."

She glanced at him again, and then stared at the ground in front of her. She wasn't scared now. He remembered that she had always been that way, even back when he had stopped at the Riley cabin with a quarter of meat or something from the Grant garden. She wasn't frightened once they started talking.

"I was real fond of your Ma, too," Laurie said. "I've been thinking about her and wishing she was here so I could talk to her. I need her advice. I guess I just don't know much about being a wife."

"Then don't be," he said. "Not now anyway. That's why I wanted to talk to you. Don't marry Duke Rome."

She didn't say anything for a moment, then she whispered, "I'd hoped you'd be happy for me. I want to be Duke's wife. I want my own home."

"You won't have it if you marry him," Kirby said. "I know him, Laurie. He's not good enough for you."

"Oh, you're wrong," she said. "I'm not good enough for him. I'm surprised you're saying that. He's got money. He promised to build or buy a cabin for us as soon as we reach Denver."

"He won't keep that promise," Kirby said. "I tell you I know him. He's not a man to hang onto his money. Sure, he's got some now from the sale of his farm, but he hasn't had much chance to spend it since we started. He will when he gets to Denver. He'll be broke in a week."

She walked beside him for several minutes without

saying a word, her gaze on the ground, then she wiped her eyes. "I am going to marry him, Kirby. I've just got to. I can't go on living with Papa and being cold and miserable all the time and wondering where my next meal is coming from. You don't know how it's been, Kirby. I think we would have starved to death in Kansas if it hadn't been for you and your folks."

"Wait," he said. "Wait till spring anyway. Maybe you can find work. When I get to Denver, I'll help you."

"Thank you, Kirby. In most things I'd take your advice, but not on this. Whatever happens to me after I marry Duke, I won't be any worse off than if I'd stayed with Papa."

He nodded, telling himself he had played God long enough. Dave Thorn had been right. Kirby didn't have God's wisdom. He hadn't spent his life living with Sam Riley the way Laurie had, either.

"You're eighteen," Kirby said. "You're old enough to do whatever you feel you have to do. I hope I'm wrong about Duke." He paused and dropped a hand on her shoulder. "Just one thing, Laurie. If it doesn't work out with Duke, or if you're ever in trouble and need help, come to me. Will you do that?"

She nodded, tears running down her cheeks. "I'll remember," she whispered. "Thank you, Kirby. You'd better go now. I'll catch up with the wagon in a minute."

He mounted and rode toward the head of the wagon train, not looking back. He had never been as sorry for anyone as he was for Laurie. She had two bad choices and maybe she was making the better of the two.

He pulled in beside the Thorn wagon. Liz said,

"You're looking downright seedy, Kirby. What's wrong?"

"I've been talking to Laurie," he said. "She's bound to marry Duke. The way she sees it, she couldn't be worse off with him than she is with her father. I guess she thinks her life might be better."

"Who's to say?" Liz asked. "You'n me both think she'll be worse off, but we don't really know for sure."

"That's what I keep telling myself," Kirby said.

Dave Thorn turned in his saddle, calling, "You'll camp there, Liz. Yonder in those cottonwoods."

Liz Thorn swung the wagon off the road and drove toward the creek, Kirby riding alongside until she stopped. He sat his saddle as the train rolled by. He raised his hand to Suzy and later to Laurie, then the wagons were past. For a time he stared at them, their white tops bobbing and lurching like a long line of ships plowing through a rough sea, and he wondered if he would ever see Laurie again.

"You can unhitch," Liz called. "Al won't be needing you. Looks like he won't even be along with the horse herd for a while."

Kirby stepped down, thinking that within the next few hours the people who had left Linn County and had been together for more than a month would scatter out. He didn't worry about Suzy. She had her brother Bill, and anyhow, she was the kind of person who could always look out for herself. But Laurie wasn't. In spite of her age, Laurie was a frightened child who needed someone to look after her with tenderness and love. And the brutal truth was she had no one.

SEVEN

KIRBY found a cottonwood drift log beside the bank of Cherry Creek. He spent the rest of the afternoon working up enough wood to keep Liz Thorn in fuel for several days. He needed to be doing something, for he was irritated at this delay. Thinking back over his conversation with Dave Thorn about working for him, he wondered how he had managed to get himself boxed in like this.

He had things to do in Denver, but here he was, camped beside Cherry Creek with Liz and Al McCoy. He didn't have the slightest idea how long he would be here, so he fiercely attacked the log that had been brought downstream by some ancient flood and then had bleached here on the bank for years. Cottonwood was not good fuel, but the wood was dry and provided enough heat for Liz to cook a meal.

He worked till he was exhausted and sweat was pouring down his lean body. He slipped on his coat and carried the wood to the camp where Liz was finishing supper. Piling it up beside the fire, he spread a canvas over it so it wouldn't get wet. Fat snowflakes drifted slowly to the earth. The wind had died down so it didn't seem as cold as it had earlier in the day.

Coffee made a tantalizing smell as Liz said, "Holler at Al, will you, Kirby? Supper's ready."

Kirby slid down the steep bank to the creek and washed. When he climbed back to the top, he yelled at McCoy, who had been working on a crude corral all

47

afternoon. When McCoy dropped his ax and joined Kirby, he said, "That ought to hold 'em if nothing scares 'em. If something does, they'll go sailing across them top poles like they wasn't there, but they're not a spooky bunch, so I don't figger I'll have any trouble."

"You must think we're going to be here a while," Kirby said.

McCoy nodded. "We might be. Whether Dave buys a stable or builds one, it's gonna take time. Looks to me like we'll be right here till he finds what he wants, 'cause I can herd 'em on the grass in the daytime. That don't cost nothing, so it'll be a hell of a lot cheaper to keep 'em out here than board 'em in town."

Kirby nodded and fell into step with McCoy. Resentment grew in him as he squatted beside the fire and ate supper. He didn't particularly like McCoy, a lean-jawed, tobacco-chewing Missourian who seemed to have no interest in anything except horses. He talked very little, and as soon as he finished eating, he rose and went back to the corral.

Kirby watched him until he disappeared into the snow that was coming down hard now. McCoy never mentioned politics, so Kirby didn't know how he felt, but coming from Missouri, he was probably a proslavery man who considered an abolitionist worse than a horse thief. He glanced at Liz, who was huddled on the other side of the fire, a blanket held around her shoulders.

"Liz, we can't stay here," Kirby said. "We may have a foot of snow on the ground by morning. Dave wouldn't want you to stay. It's not more than five miles to Denver. Let's go—"

"No," she said sharply. "Dave wants us to stay here."

"Sure, that's what he said, but he didn't expect a storm like this."

"These early storms never amount to much," she said. "I'll be all right. I'll give you a couple of extra blankets and you sleep under the wagon."

He shook his head. "Liz, you can get sick camping out in this kind of weather. If I know Dave, it's the last thing he'd want. I don't know what he'd do if he lost you."

"I don't either," she said, smiling a little, "but if he wanted us to come into town, he'd ride back and tell us."

"Maybe it isn't snowing like this in Denver," Kirby argued. "Or maybe he can't get away."

"No, Kirby." She had never been angry or even sharp with him before, but she was now. "In the first place, we don't know we could find any rooms. In the second place, it'll be dark in an hour or so and we could get lost and be a lot worse off than we are now. In the third place, Dave told us to stay."

He filled his pipe and lighted it with a burning stick, then tossed the stick back and threw several more pieces of wood on the fire. He said, "I guess you can do what you want, Liz, but I'm going to saddle up—"

"No." She screamed the word at him, and then lowered her gaze as she struggled to control her temper. Finally she said, "I'm sorry I spoke that way, but I'm scared to stay here alone with McCoy. Dave knew you can be trusted. The last thing he said before I turned off was that McCoy could watch the horses and you'd look out for me." She swallowed and threw out her hands in a begging gesture. "Please stay, Kirby. You promised."

He started to say he hadn't promised, that Dave had simply told him this was what he would do without asking him if he would. But for some reason Liz was thoroughly frightened. She had a right to be, he thought. He didn't think McCoy was a man to be trusted, and of course there would be other men riding past the camp who might molest a woman.

"All right, Liz," Kirby said. "I'll stay."

He saw the expression of relief that was in her face. She tried to say something, but the words wouldn't come. She just sat there with her head bowed and tears running down her cheeks. A full minute passed before she was able to brush them away and look at Kirby.

"Thank you," she said in a low tone. "You scared me. I've got to stay here and I wouldn't have known what to do if you'd left me." She shivered and put her hands over the fire. "This is a hard thing to tell you, Kirby. Maybe I shouldn't."

She paused, staring at the flames, and then she shivered. She moistened her lips and went on, "I will tell you whether I should or not. I'm afraid of Dave. I know you like him. Even admire him, I guess. Well, I love him and I suppose he loves me, but we've been married almost thirty years. I know him, Kirby. I know how he thinks and feels and what he'll do. Most of the time he's a good husband, but I learned a long time ago that I had better do what he tells me. I wouldn't dare leave here before he comes back, not if there was a flood or a fire or an earthquake."

His pipe went cold in his mouth. He stared at her, unable to believe what he had heard. He had known the

Thorns only casually before he joined the wagon train, because they had lived in Fort Scott, which was south of Mound City, the town nearest to the Grant farm. But neither Kirby nor his folks had heard anything against either Dave or Liz Thorn, and Kirby had spent hours with Thorn on the trip. He had talked a great deal to Liz, too, in the evenings after supper. Kirby had always felt they had a better than average marriage, but here Liz was telling him straight out that she was afraid of Dave.

"Why do you stay married to him?" he asked finally.

"I told you I love him," she said. "Don't ask me why. I mean, I don't think there is ever an explanation of why a woman loves a man, but if she does, she stays with him no matter what happens."

"Or what he does to her?"

Liz nodded. "Or what he does to her."

He thought about Laurie Riley then. He said, "At least Dave has made a good living for you."

"Yes, he's a good provider, and that helps to put up with his. . . ." She paused, then said thoughtfully, "I guess you'd say his domineering ways. As long as I do what I know I'm supposed to, and he never leaves any doubt about that, we get along fine. In fact, I couldn't ask for a better husband."

"I was thinking about Laurie," he said. "She's bound to marry Duke. I couldn't say anything to change her. She had to get away from her father, she said. Well, I can understand that, but marrying Duke is like jumping out of a lukewarm frying pan into a hot fire."

"I guess I should have talked to her," Liz said, "but there it was, you see. Dave told me not to."

He remembered. He said rebelliously, "I wish you had anyway. If she just had another year, or even a few months, she'd know what to do."

Liz shook her head as she rose and tossed the blanket into the wagon. "I couldn't have talked to her, Kirby. Not after what Dave said. I decided he was right. After all, being married to Duke might be better than living with Sam Riley. Who are you or me to decide a thing like that?" She picked up an empty bucket and handed it to him. "Fill this for me, will you?"

He knocked his pipe out against his heel and dropped it into his pocket. Picking up the bucket, he walked to the creek. The snow was beginning to cover the ground, and he wasn't at all sure that Liz's notion about early winter storms not amounting to much was true. He thought of what she had said about Laurie and decided she was right after all. Laurie was still a child, but it was her decision just the same. If his advice was wrong and she followed it, he would be to blame for her unhappiness. Though she hadn't sounded as if she were going to change her mind anyway. . . .

He was stooping to fill the bucket, his thoughts still on Laurie, when he heard the hoofbeats of incoming horses. He straightened, the half-filled bucket in his hand. He heard the roar of a gun, then Liz's scream. He dropped the bucket and scrambled up the bank as running horses appeared from the north, vague, fast-moving shapes in the snow-filtered light.

Again a gun sounded, the tongue of flame lashing out and dying. Kirby drew his revolver and ran toward them, firing as fast as he could. There were four riders, or maybe five. He wasn't sure in the thin light. For an instant it seemed that all of them were shooting at him, bullets sounding like the darting rush of angry bees as they hummed past him. Their bullets missed, and as far as he knew, his did too.

They disappeared to the south behind the curtain of swirling snow. He holstered his empty gun, suddenly aware that Liz was still standing beside the wagon and screaming. He ran to her and put his hands on her shoulders.

"Are you all right?" She continued to scream hysterically. He shook her, asking again, "Are you all right?"

She put a hand over her mouth and stopped screaming. She stared at him, wide-eyed. He felt her tremble, and then she was able to say, "Yes, I'm all right." McCoy ran up just as Liz asked, "Are you hurt, Kirby? They were after you."

"No, they wasn't," McCoy said sharply. "They wanted the horses."

Kirby whirled on him. "How do you know? They didn't stop long enough to see if any horses were here."

"They knew," McCoy snapped back. "Everybody in the train knew the horses were here. It'd be all over Denver by now."

"I didn't hear you do any shooting," Kirby said.

"They was here and gone afore I knowed what was happening," McCoy said glibly, as if he had rehearsed his speech and knew exactly what he was going to say. "Besides, I was waiting for 'em to make a try for the horses. I didn't want my gun empty if they did."

"I don't think they were after the horses," Kirby said.

"Maybe they knew there was a woman in camp."

"Maybe they did," McCoy snapped, "and you drove 'em off."

"Next time you'd better give me a hand—"

"I look after the horses," McCoy said. "You look after Miz Thorn."

He wheeled and strode away. Kirby turned to Liz. "Why would they be after me?"

"They weren't," she said as if suddenly she were very tired. "You were right. They'd heard there was a woman in camp. Now you see why you can't leave."

"Yeah, I see," he said. "I'll go get the water."

As he walked back to the creek to where he had left the bucket, he wondered why she had said they were after him and then changed it to agree with what he had said. She might have been right at first, he thought, for there were men in Denver who wanted to kill him, but Liz Thorn would have no way of knowing that. And how could they know this quickly?

EIGHT

DAVE Thorn did not return to camp until Sunday afternoon, October 6. Once Kirby made up his mind that he had to stay, and the hit-and-run attack on that first evening had made up his mind for him, he had been able to accept what he told Liz was his "exile."

After the first snowy night, the weather turned warm and the days were very pleasant. He had nothing to do except bring water from the creek and keep enough wood on hand for Liz's needs. He lounged around camp, napping during the day and staying awake all night.

He had a feeling that the men who had made the attack might try again. Besides, a good many people went by on the road, families and single men in covered wagons and men on horseback. Few stopped to talk, for now that they were so close to Denver, most of them felt compelled to finish their journey as soon as they could.

Kirby told Liz to wake him if anyone stopped during the day. At night he made his bed some distance from the wagon and changed the place every night. But nothing happened. Kirby had a sense of urgency about what he had to do in Denver, but, much to his surprise, he found himself enjoying the long, lazy days.

When Thorn rode into camp, Liz hugged and kissed him as if she had never expected him to return, then she cried a little and he patted her on the back and said he'd bought a nice cabin for her and the camping days were over. Kirby shook hands with him, but McCoy didn't say a word. He took the reins from Thorn and led the big black away.

Liz poured a cup of coffee and gave it to Thorn as he squatted beside the fire. He hadn't shaved for several days, and his clothes were dirty. Kirby thought he seemed tired and years older than when he'd left a few days ago.

"I've got a lot to tell you," Thorn said. "I don't know quite where to begin, but I can tell you mighty quick that I'm glad I left you here, Liz. Denver is a tough town. You won't be out on the street after dark. When Kirby and I are gone, you keep the cabin locked."

"It can't be that bad," Liz said incredulously.

"It seemed that bad to me," Thorn said. "I watched a hanging yesterday, a young fellow named James Gordon who had murdered a man. Very brutally, they say. I guess his friends were trying to free him up to the very last. Even though I was new in town, it struck me that this was actually a test of strength between the lawless element and the decent citizens. I guess you'd say the decent citizens won. At least this man Gordon paid for the murder he committed. Whether the toughs learned anything from it is something we will have to find out."

He finished his coffee, and handed the tin cup back to Liz. "I bought a barn. It's not a big one, but it'll do. I don't expect to run much competition to the Elephant Corral. The barn belonged to a man who was lynched by the Stranglers a few weeks ago, so there were some legal matters to be worked out before I could take the barn."

"The Stranglers?" Liz looked at him in horror. "What kind of a country have we come to, Dave?"

"They call the Vigilantes the Stranglers," Thorn said. "I'm afraid I asked the same question during the hanging. The occasion was a holiday for some of the men. It seemed like watching a man die a horrible death gave them pleasure."

Thorn fished his pipe out of his pocket and loaded it, then lifted his gaze to Liz's face. "You see, the people here have had to establish their own system of law and order. It struck me that the rough element, the ones they called the Bummers, form an unusually large percentage of the total population. This was one reason the Vigilantes were organized."

He reached for a light from the fire. When he had his

pipe going, he went on, "I don't hold with the Vigilante way of doing things, but we have to admit that they did a necessary job in California. I suppose they did here. There have been a number of lynchings which have been laid to them. At first they had a big organization, about a hundred, I understand, but there was a leak. Now a small group of ten men do the work, and they say the Bummers are a little more careful."

"The Gordon hanging had nothing to do with the Stranglers?" Kirby asked.

"Well, it was all open and aboveboard," Thorn answered. "He was publicly tried and had some good lawyers defending him, including Park McClure, the postmaster. I was told the court leaned over backwards to give him a fair trial."

Thorn took the pipe out of his mouth and studied it. He went on thoughtfully, "It's a pretty complicated situation. The decent citizens had to do something, or the Bummers would have taken the town over. On the other hand, we have ten men who can meet and decide my fate. Or yours, Kirby. If they charge you with a crime, you don't have a public trial. You have no right to defend yourself. You don't have a lawyer. They simply take you out and hang you, and by God, nobody else knows who did it or exactly why."

"If some of these men get it in for you," Kirby said, "they can hang you and claim you're a criminal whether you are or not?"

"That's the size of it," Thorn said. "I don't mind telling you it's a little scary."

"Let's go back to Fort Scott," Liz said.

"No, we're here and we'll stay, but I thought I'd better lay it out for both of you so you'll know how it is." Thorn puffed a moment, then said around the pipestem, "I think Denver is past the worst, so maybe the Vigilantes will disband."

Watching Thorn, Kirby sensed again the uncertainty he had noticed that first night they camped on Cherry Creek. There seemed little reason to worry about the Vigilantes if a man ran a clean business and stayed out of trouble. For the first time the thought occurred to Kirby that maybe Dave Thorn had something in mind beside running a clean business, but that was ridiculous, and Kirby dismissed the idea immediately.

"Well, I guess we'd better talk about our future," Thorn said, suddenly cheerful as if he had dissipated his fears by expressing them. "The cabin has an attic room where you can sleep, Kirby. Liz and me will sleep downstairs. There's a room in the barn where McCoy can stay. We need to keep at least one man there all the time. As long as the weather stays good, Kirby, you'll be hauling hay for me. There is some in the barn, and I made arrangements to buy more from a farmer north of town who has a place on the South Platte."

Thorn rose and stretched. "We probably won't do much business this winter, but come spring when men start heading out of town for the mines, we'll be able to rent every horse we've got."

"Dave, did you know we were set upon by a gang of four or five men?" Kirby asked.

Surprised, Thorn said, "What do you mean, set upon?"

"They rode past here like they were headed somewhere in a hurry," Kirby said. "They used up considerable lead as they went by. I was on the creek when I heard a shot. Liz screamed, and when I got on the bank and started shooting at them, they shot back at me. Liz said they were after me and I thought they were after her and McCoy claims they were after the horses."

Thorn pulled at his beard, his gaze darting to his wife, then swung back to Kirby's face. "That's a hell of a note. I thought you'd all be safer out here than in town." He shook his head. "No reason for them to be after you, and they wouldn't be shooting at Liz if they aimed to rape her. Besides, there are a lot of prostitutes in town, so I don't see any reason for them to ride out here and attack a decent woman. No, I'm inclined to agree with Al. This many horses could be a gold mine."

He started to walk to the corral, then stopped and turned back. "I've got some bad news, Kirby. I almost forgot to tell you. Sam Riley was shot and killed the first night he was in Denver."

"What?" Kirby shook his head, so hard hit by this he could not believe it. "Why?"

"You know how Sam was when he drank too much," Thorn said. "Claimed to be a great abolitionist and a conductor on the underground railroad and all. He wandered into a place called the Criterion—seems it's a hangout for men who have Southern sympathies. He started talking and he got plugged. From what I heard, he was told to shut up and get out. When he didn't, a man told him he was worse than a horse thief, and knocked him down. Sam tried for his gun, and the other fellow shot him in the stomach. He died before morning."

"What happened to Laurie?" Liz asked.

"You can guess," Thorn said. "Duke Rome married her. I don't think he aimed to yet, but he couldn't do much else. They were married by the Reverend Chivington who is a presiding elder of the Methodist Episcopal church, so Laurie got it done up brown just like she wanted it. Duke sold Sam's team and wagon and everything they didn't need, and then they struck out for the mines. I don't know where they went."

"Poor Laurie," Liz murmured. "I hoped she would have a little time."

Kirby turned and walked aimlessly away from the wagon. He wished he knew where Laurie and Duke had gone. Maybe he could find out when he reached Denver. If he did, he would look them up. If Duke hadn't treated her right. . . .

Suddenly Kirby remembered thinking that he or Duke might kill the other. Now he had a strange, almost overpowering sensation of looking ahead in time and being certain that it would happen. If Duke Rome abused Laurie, he would kill the man, and Duke was the kind who would abuse a woman.

NINE

THEY reached Denver before noon on Monday, Liz driving the wagon, Kirby helping Thorn and McCoy with the horses. They left the horses with McCoy in the corral behind the barn, which was on Blake Street about two blocks from Cherry Creek. Then, with Thorn leading, they turned left one block on G Street and right on Wazee and a moment later came to a cabin.

Thorn motioned for Liz to stop. He dismounted and, bowing, made a sweeping gesture with his hat. "Alight and enter your palatial abode," he said.

For a moment Liz didn't move. She sat motionless, staring at the log cabin with its two small windows on the street side. Kirby thought she was going to cry. He judged that they had been reasonably well off during most of their married life. He knew that they'd had a comfortable home in Fort Scott. Now, to move into a log cabin in a rough frontier town like Denver was almost more than she could bear.

But she didn't break down. She stepped to the ground, and smiled at Thorn as she said, "You always carry me across the threshold when we move into a palatial abode."

"Of course," he said, and, sweeping her into his arms, carried her into the cabin.

Kirby remained where he was, not wanting to intrude upon their privacy. Liz would get over her disappointment, he thought. The cabin looked better than many of the shacks he had seen since he'd ridden into town.

He noticed a number of cottonwood trees on the other side of Cherry Creek in what had been the old town of Auraria but was now a part of Denver. There were no trees on this side except to the north where a number of large cottonwoods marked the South Platte bottom. Dust lay deep in the street, which had not been graded. On rainy days the mud would be ankle-deep.

Denver was just about what he had expected, a rough, sprawling frontier town. He had no idea how many people lived here and in the mining camps, but he wished he knew. The big question in his mind was when the Pikes Peak country would be recognized by Congress as a territory, and then whether there would be enough population for it to become a state. He could not make a guess about the latter, but he was convinced from what he had seen already that Congress would soon be forced to organize a territory.

Presently Thorn came out of the cabin. He said, "She's not happy. It wasn't worth it."

"What wasn't?"

Startled, Thorn's face turned red as he glanced at Kirby. "I was talking to hear my tongue rattle. I shouldn't bother you with family trouble. It's just that we were well situated in Fort Scott, and we should have stayed."

Liz had told Kirby she was scared of her husband, but now it struck him that Thorn was scared of her. Kirby said, "Give her some time, Dave. In another year you can build a fine house right here in Denver."

"Sure," Thorn said as he climbed to the wagon seat. "I'll pull in close to the front door and we'll unload. She'll feel better when she gets her knickknacks around her."

She did, too. Kirby was surprised how much better Liz felt by late afternoon when the wagon was unloaded. The interior of the cabin was one big room, with a lean-to on the back that was a small bedroom. The attic room upstairs was too low for Kirby to stand, but it would be adequate for the few hours of sleeping he would do each night.

Kirby tied the saddle horses behind the wagon, and drove to the barn. He stayed there while McCoy went to the cabin for his supper, then McCoy came back to the barn while Kirby went to the cabin.

"It will take a little time to get everything put away," Liz told Kirby, "but when I do, we'll be as snug as a bug in a rug."

Kirby glanced at Thorn who had finished eating and was leaning back in his chair and loading his pipe. Kirby thought about saying that Liz's disposition had improved, but decided against it. He felt a tension between them that was unusual. Presently Thorn said, "I'll go help McCoy get squared away for the night," and left the cabin.

When Kirby had finished eating, he leaned back in his chair, and filled his pipe. He said, "Liz, you told me you were scared of Dave, but it seems to me there's times when he's scared of you. I don't savvy."

She darted a glance at him, then she shrugged and laughed. "Oh, I get the best of him once in a while, but it doesn't change anything."

Kirby spent an hour exploring some of the arenas of joy that evening. He was impressed by the Criterion, which was presided over by Charley Harrison, a handsome man with a beautiful silky beard. He was the most famous gambler and gunman in Colorado, and now, looking at him, Kirby understood why.

Harrison was immaculately clad in black, and carried two pearl-handled .41 Colts. He moved easily through

63

the crowd, stopping now and then to speak with someone he knew. To Kirby, who had heard so much about the man and had looked forward to seeing him, Harrison possessed an elegant dignity that set him apart from the rough-looking men who filled the saloon.

Kirby considered questioning Harrison or one of the bartenders about Sam Riley's death. He decided against it, knowing he would be a marked man soon enough, and it would be the height of stupidity to call attention to himself before he had to. Besides, Sam Riley could not be brought to life no matter who had killed him.

When he returned to the cabin, Thorn was waiting for him. Liz had gone to bed. Thorn asked sharply, "Where have you been?"

Kirby held his answer for a moment, looking directly at Thorn. The man's cheeks were flushed, and a pulse was hammering in his temples. He had no right to ask questions and even less to lose his temper. Still, Kirby wanted no trouble with him if he could avoid it, so he said gently, "Dave, I know that jobs and beds are hard to find in Denver, but if I have to tell you where I am every hour, I'll start looking."

"I'm sorry." Thorn threw out a hand in an involuntary gesture. "I didn't aim to pry into your business, but damn it, I got back just a little while ago and found Liz alone. I was worried about her, after it was too late, I mean. I'd have come on home sooner if I'd known you weren't staying."

"We can't be with her all the time," Kirby said. "You'll have to give her a gun."

"She's got a Colt .32," Thorn said. "You're right. We

can't be with her all the time. She'll just have to defend herself if she has to."

"I don't mind telling you where I was," Kirby said. "I wanted a look at Charley Harrison, so I had a drink in the Criterion."

"He's bad," Thorn said moodily. "They claim he has eleven notches on one side of a gun barrel for the men he's killed, and three on the other side for the women."

Kirby grinned. "I've heard that story too. I guess every man who's been out here and gone back home has to tell about Charley Harrison. The way I heard it, he's supposed to have said that three women equal one man, so it adds up to a jury that's waiting in hell to try him."

Thorn nodded. "I guess somebody starts the yarns about Harrison, and they keep adding to it."

"You know," Kirby said thoughtfully, "he didn't look like a man who would notch his guns. I don't believe it."

"Maybe not," Thorn said, "but don't start anything with Harrison unless you're fixing to cash in your chips."

"I'm not quite ready yet," Kirby said as he turned toward the ladder that led to the attic room upstairs.

Kirby stretched out on the pallet that Liz had put down for him, and thought of the Bummers and the Vigilantes who were also known as the Stranglers, of Charley Harrison who openly sympathized with the South, of the Elephant Corral and the Criterion and the other gaming places where a man could lose his last cent in a matter of minutes at faro or three-card monte.

This was Denver, wild and turbulent and exciting, Denver where in the end the decision would be made as to whether the Pikes Peak country would be free or slave. He was here to help make that decision. Now, staring into the darkness, he wondered how soon the Brotherhood would get in touch with him, and what he would do if no contact was made.

TEN

KIRBY started hauling hay Tuesday morning. He found that by leaving Denver right after breakfast, he could reach the farm where Dave Thorn had bought the hay, load, and return by noon. He forked the hay from the rack into the space in the rear of the building that served as a mow, and then by eating a quick dinner, he had time for another load in the afternoon.

His evenings were free after supper, so he cruised along Larimer and Blake streets, stopping at the Criterion and the Elephant Corral and other saloons. Only occasionally did he cross Cherry Creek to what had been Auraria. It seemed to him that the original Denver townsite was gaining on what had been a rival settlement, so he spent most of his time there. Besides, the Elephant Corral fascinated him, and each evening he would spend an hour in its gambling saloon and not more than a few minutes in the other gaming places.

The Elephant Corral had everything for the traveler. He could drive into the corral proper and leave his wagon there while his horses were taken to a barn that was on one side. He could then go into the saloon, confident his property would not be stolen. The chances were he never gave a thought to the fact that a worse fate might wait for him in the saloon where several hundred men had gathered to drink and buck the tiger. A number of bedrooms were in the back, the furniture crude, the mattresses filled with grass.

From what Kirby heard, gambling went on day and night, and he could not help wondering what happened to men who went broke. It was too late in the season to go back to the mining camps, the passage across the plains to the States was expensive, and jobs were scarce in Denver. The situation encouraged lawlessness, and Kirby didn't doubt that some of the men who couldn't find work turned to crime who would not ordinarily have done so.

He wondered about Duke Rome and Laurie, but he didn't hear anything about them. He wondered, too, where Suzy Jones and her brother Bill had got to, but he didn't worry about them as he did about Laurie. Duke might very well have lost every cent he had at faro or any of the other games.

That could have been the reason Duke had left Denver, but Bill Jones was not that kind of man. Kirby expected to see him some evening, probably in the Criterion, because Jones was a proslavery man, but he didn't. Neither Thorn nor McCoy had heard anything about Bill or Suzy.

As Kirby drifted around town, he learned to recognize some of the better-known residents of Denver, including the famous William Byers, whom Kirby had heard quoted back in Kansas. Byers had earned his reputation of Fighting Editor, and had found that it was to his advantage to carry two Colt revolvers.

There were many others, men who had their fingers on the pulsebeat of Denver's hectic life, but none of them seemed to be aware that Kirby Grant had come to town. Somewhere in this crowd of men who jostled and elbowed one another on Denver's boardwalks was one who wanted to see him. Perhaps Kirby had passed him a dozen times, neither knowing the other.

During the second week he had a feeling he was being followed. He wasn't sure when he first noticed that the same man appeared too often every time he stepped into a saloon and stood watching a game, a man who remained at a nearby table ostensibly interested in the game that was being played there but keeping his gaze covertly on Kirby all the time. A rather faceless kind of man, with nothing to set him apart from the hundreds of bewhiskered miners who crowded the streets every night, he would invariably appear in the next saloon soon after Kirby entered.

By the second Friday that he was in Denver, Kirby was certain that the man showed up too often for it to be a coincidence. He decided to have it out with the fellow.

Kirby left the Criterion about ten and followed Larimer Street to Cherry Creek. There he crossed the bridge, and moved back into the darkness until he heard a man's steps. When the man came opposite, Kirby lunged forward and caught him around the throat with a forearm which he pressed tightly as he jammed his gun barrel into the man's back.

"I'll give you ten seconds to tell me who you are," Kirby said, "and why you're following me, or I'll squeeze the trigger, and you will have two short backbones instead of a long one."

The man twisted and squirmed and gurgled, and finally Kirby realized that he couldn't talk. Releasing the pressure on his throat, Kirby said, "Now you can speak your piece."

"I was fixing to rob you," the man said. "I'm hungry and broke, and I've been waiting for a chance to get you out alone somewhere."

"You're lying," Kirby said. "Who put you up to following me?"

"Nobody," the fellow said desperately. "I haven't eaten for three days. I'll rob somebody and kill him if I have to before I'll starve to death."

"I say you're lying." Kirby pressed the muzzle of his revolver harder than ever against the man's spine. "Somebody's paying you to trail me. Who?"

"Nobody," the man whined. "I keep telling you. I'm just hungry."

"All right." Kirby holstered his gun. "Don't let me catch you following me again."

He drew his arm away from the man's throat and stepped back, his hand on the butt of his revolver, but there was no fight in the man. He plunged away into the darkness and a moment later the sound of his pounding boots faded and died. Kirby tried, but he could not believe the man was a simple thief.

The following noon, as Kirby was forking the last of his load of hay into the mow, he heard someone come into the barn from the street and looked up just as a man called, "Thorn."

69

Dave Thorn and McCoy had gone to the cabin for dinner and Kirby was alone. He yelled, "Thorn will be back in a few minutes," and went on pitching hay.

The man strolled along the runway, glancing around. When he reached the end of the hayrack, he said, "I wanted to talk to Thorn or McCoy about renting a saddle horse."

"They'll soon be back," Kirby said.

He pitched the last forkful of hay from the wagon to the mow. He stepped down, thinking it was time for Thorn to be back when the impression came to him that this man was vaguely familiar. He started to turn away when recognition came. This was the man who had been following him. He would have recognized him sooner except that his coming here was completely unexpected. Too, the light inside the barn was thin. He made a grab for the pitchfork as the man said in a low tone, "Tonight at eight. First cabin on the right after you cross the Larimer Street bridge. Don't let anyone follow you."

Kirby froze as the man walked rapidly away. His people had spotted him, all right, and he had been under observation. They hadn't wanted to claim him until they were sure he was the kind who would be useful to them, and not the Sam Riley type who would shoot off his mouth and get himself killed and maybe give away some fraternal secrets in the process.

The afternoon dragged for Kirby. Usually he finished pitching his second load of hay into the mow, unharnessed, and ate his supper well before eight o'clock. For some reason one thing after another went wrong today. McCoy was slow getting back to the barn. Then when

70

Kirby reached the cabin he found that Liz had let the fire go out, and he had to wait until she warmed up his food. He had intended to change his clothes, but it was five minutes after eight and he could not take the time.

Thorn was sitting by the stove smoking when Kirby rose from the table. He said, "Kirby, you'll have to take a shift at the barn tonight. McCoy's been there every evening and he says he wants to cut his wolf loose tonight."

"I can't," Kirby said. "I have other plans."

He didn't have time to discuss it with Thorn, but when he reached the door, he found Thorn there ahead of him. "You listen to me, son," Thorn said. "You're supposed to be taking my orders. You'll do it if you want to keep your job."

Precious seconds ticked away as Kirby fought his temper. He stood within a step of Thorn, his pulse hammering in his temples. He saw the anger that was in Thorn's face and knew it would take very little to push this to a fight.

"Dave, don't shove me," Kirby said. "I thought you knew me better than that."

"And I thought you knew me better than you seem to," Thorn flung at him. "This is the first time I've asked you to take a turn in the barn. It's only fair to let McCoy have an evening off."

"Any other evening and I would have agreed with you," Kirby said, "but you didn't mention it before and I have a date. I'll move out in the morning and you can find a man who will take your orders."

He pushed past Thorn and left the cabin, not sure for a

moment whether Thorn would attempt to stop him or not. He heard Liz say, "Don't, Dave." He kept walking, not looking back, so he did not know what Thorn had started to do.

He reached G Street and turned left. When he came to Larimer, he remembered what the man had said about not letting anyone follow him. He continued on Larimer as far as the Wallingford and Murphy store, then stepped into the darkness beside the building and waited, but no one walked past the store for the minute or two that he stood there.

Satisfied that no one was following him, he went on past the Criterion, crossed F Street, and kept a steady pace, passing the Graham Drug Store and the Apollo Theater. He was out of the crowd now, and paused again, moving off the boardwalk into the dry weeds of a vacant lot. He listened, but all he heard were the usual crowd noises in front of the Apollo Theater.

He crossed the bridge, remembering the cabin that was built between Cherry Creek and Front Street. It was very close to the bank, so close that a wrong step in the darkness could send a man tumbling into the sandy bed of the stream.

From the street the cabin appeared to be dark, but when he reached the front door he saw a faint line of light under the thick shade that covered the window. He knocked three times and waited. Presently he heard footsteps move to the door.

A moment of silence followed. For a time the possibility of treachery crossed his mind. It seemed impossible, yet he knew that in a game as deadly as this, anything was possible. From inside the cabin a man said, "John."

"Brown," Kirby said.

"Harper's," the man said.

"Ferry," Kirby said.

Kirby knocked three times again, then the door opened and the man who had come to the barn that noon stood there, smiling. He said, "Come in, Brother Grant," and held out his hand. "I'm Martin Kane. Welcome to the Denver chapter of the Free Soilers."

Kirby stepped inside and shook the man's hand. "I'm glad to be here after—" He stopped, his heart beating so crazily that he thought it might jump out of his chest. Three men sat at a table in the middle of the room. One of them was Bill Jones.

For the short moment that he stared at Jones, who sat grinning at him, the thought of treachery was the only one in his mind. He reached for his gun, knowing he had stepped into a trap.

ELEVEN

THREE things happened instantaneously, all of them coming so quickly that it took a moment for Kirby to sort them out in his mind. Martin Kane grabbed Kirby's wrist just as his revolver cleared leather and held it at his side so that he could not bring it into firing position. Bill Jones jumped to his feet and held his hands up so Kirby could see he was not going for his gun. A door in the back of the room opened and Suzy stood there, smiling until she saw what was happening;

then she called, "Kirby," and ran across the room to him.

"Bill is one of us," Kane said. "I should have told you."

"No, I should have told him a long time ago," Suzy said gravely, as she took Kirby's arm. "Bill wanted me to tell him the night we camped on Cherry Creek, but I got mad at him. The next thing I knew he walked off, so I just went to bed."

Her brother grinned sourly. "I had a hell of a fight on my hands, all because my hot-tempered sis got mad and didn't do what she was supposed to."

Kirby backed to the log wall and leaned against it, wiping the sweat from his forehead. Suzy tugged at his arm, saying, "Let's sit down, Kirby. I suppose you're mad, but you've got to listen anyhow."

"I'm not mad," Kirby said. "I guess I'm kind of confused."

"Nobody can blame you." Kane motioned toward the table. "I want you to meet our brothers."

Two men, strangers to Kirby, were seated at the table. They rose as Kirby walked to them, Suzy still holding his left arm possessively. The tall one, a gangling man about fifty who had inordinately long arms and legs, held out his hand.

"Kirby, meet Randy Curl," Kane said. "Randy, this is Kirby Grant."

"Mighty pleased to meet you," Curl said. "I was ready to hit the floor a minute ago. You went off like a bear trap. Looked to me like you was gonna sprinkle some lead around the room before Martin could get you cooled off."

"I'm glad he stopped me," Kirby said, instinctively liking the man.

"The other one is Arch Bland," Kane said. "He knows your friend Montgomery."

Bland seemed to Kirby to be out of place in this group. He was short and stocky, probably thirty years old, with a wiry black beard and flashing eyes that bored into Kirby as he said, "Glad to meet you, Grant. The way you got your gun out of the holster convinced me we can use you."

"Sure we can use him," Bill Jones said, slapping Kirby on the back. "He's a good man. I watched him all the way from Linn County to Cherry Creek and I know."

"How's the colonel?" Bland asked.

For a moment Kirby didn't know whom he was talking about, and his confusion apparently was mirrored in his face, for Bland added impatiently, "Montgomery. Colonel James Montgomery."

"Oh, he's fine," Kirby said. "I saw him about a week before I left."

"Still the great crusader, I suppose," Bland said. "Still filled with the Holy Spirit directing him to strike hard at the Border Ruffians."

"He hasn't changed," Kirby said stiffly, not sure whether Bland's irony was meant to bait him or not.

"He never will," Kane said. "Well, sit down, Grant. We have a great deal to talk about."

Kirby sat down on a bench beside Bill Jones, Suzy sitting on the other side of him, her hand holding his left one. She had a proprietary air about her as if wanting everyone to know he was her man. She was assuming too much, he thought, yet when he glanced down at her, and she looked up and met his gaze, smiling at him, he could not keep from thinking that she was an uncommonly pretty and vibrant girl.

When he thought of Duke Rome and Dave Thorn, he felt alone and friendless. In those moments the need of having someone to love and to love him pressed upon him, but there was always the balancing thought that it would be wrong to let it happen now.

He turned his gaze suddenly to Martin Kane, who had taken a seat at the end of the table, his eyes fixed on Suzy's face. Kirby said more explosively than he intended, "I have something to say, and I have an explanation coming."

"You do indeed," Kane said. "Do you want your say first?"

"We'd better remind him of a few things," Bland broke in. "We are free to say anything to each other that we want to say, but nothing . . . absolutely nothing . . . must ever be told outside these four walls about what was said or who was here."

"That's right," Kane agreed, "but since you belong to the Brotherhood in Kansas, you know these things. All Arch wants is to remind you of them."

"And you also need to be reminded that if anyone breaks this rule," Bland went on, "he pays with his life. You or me or even Miss Jones will execute the guilty party if he is appointed to carry out the death sentence."

For a moment Kirby had a nagging doubt about his wisdom in coming here. He doubted if he could carry out such a sentence if he were appointed the executioner.

He had taken the same oath in Kansas that these men had taken. Probably Suzy had taken it, too. He moistened his lips, knowing that if he were told to kill Suzy, he would refuse to do it regardless of what happened to him.

He could walk out now before anything was said and be a free man; then he realized that this was foolish thinking. It was too late. He would never be a free man again, at least not until this trouble was over. He knew who was here. They would kill him before they would let him leave if he got up and walked toward the door claiming that he was no longer bound by the oath.

He moistened his lips again. "I understand. I'll have my say first."

"Good," Kane nodded. "Go ahead."

"First I'd like to say why I'm here," Kirby said. "Maybe I ought to call it a statement of belief."

Kane smiled, his eyes turning to Suzy and then coming back to Kirby. "It might do all of us good if we made such a statement. I assure you that we will be interested in hearing yours."

Kirby hesitated, suddenly feeling like a callow youth who was impelled to talk about a problem that older men understood perfectly. He had thought of Martin Kane as a faceless man, one of dozens of miners who walked the Denver streets every day. Now he realized he had been wrong, that Kane who obviously was the leader of this group was a strong man, perhaps a ruthless man, one who could play whatever role he chose.

"First, I believe the Union as we have known it since George Washington's time must be preserved regardless of the cost in lives or property," Kirby said. "If the Republicans win, and I think they will, some of the Southern states will try to secede just as they are threatening. This must not be permitted."

"We'll support that part of your statement," Kane said.

"The second part has to do with what I don't believe in," Kirby went on. "The slavery issue is a minor one in my opinion. I'm called an abolitionist and my father is called one, and both of us have helped runaway slaves escape. I'm not sorry about what I've done, but I don't hold with James Montgomery and Doc Jennison and other jayhawkers who raid the homes of proslavery people and steal their horses and burn their buildings and even murder—"

"You have to fight fire with fire," Archibald Bland broke in heatedly. "Look what the Border Ruffians did to us. Montgomery is a great patriot—"

"Arch." Kane tapped the table with his fist. "You're out of order."

Bland leaned back on his bench, his face red. He had meant to bait, Kirby thought. Bland was a fanatic, another John Brown unable to think beyond the immediate problem of setting the slaves free. Like Brown, and the jayhawker leaders such as Montgomery and Jennison, Bland would give his life and sacrifice others as well if he thought it would contribute toward freeing the slaves.

"Go on," Kane said, nodding at Kirby.

"I'm done, I guess," Kirby said.

"I think not," Kane said softly, his gaze on Kirby's face. "You must have a third plank in your platform. The rest of us do. That's why we're here." He hesitated, Kirby looking at him, puzzled, then Kane went on, "You see, none of us can keep the Southern states from seceding, but we believe there is something we can do."

Kirby grinned. "Why, yes, I do have a third plank. I will do anything I can as long as it is within the law to keep Jefferson Territory from coming into the Union as a slave state."

"Good," Kane said.

"It ain't good enough," Bland broke in. "We'd better have it understood that the law——"

Kane tapped the table sharply with his fist, his face showing his irritation. "Arch, you are out of order again. This is the second time. You will lose your place at this table if it happens a third time."

"It won't," Bland muttered. "I just thought——"

"I know exactly what you thought." Kane nodded at Kirby. "I'm afraid you will have to amend your third plank slightly. You haven't been in Denver long, but those of us who have realize that the law is not much help in these times. Much of the lawlessness that has plagued Denver from the beginning is due to the fact that we have two groups, one Northern and one Southern in sympathy."

"I understand that," Kirby said.

"But I think you do not understand that the law out here is what we make it," Kane went on. "If it had not been for the Vigilantes and their harsh methods, the Bummers would be in control of the local government and many men of substance would be dead by now, or robbed of their possessions. Men like Charley Harrison and Park McClure and Major John Moore will go a long ways to make this a slave state. At present they spy on us and we spy on them, but the day will come when we will have to fight and we'll kill, because we are fighting a war right here just as surely as you and your father and Colonel James Montgomery fought it back there in Linn County."

Kirby nodded, understanding that too. "I can do what has to be done when the time comes."

"I'm sure you can," Kane said.

"I'd like to tell him something," Bill Jones said. "The sooner he hears it the better."

"I think so, too," Kane said gravely.

Jones turned to Kirby. He said, "We have reason to believe that Dave Thorn is on the other side, and that he came here for the opposite reasons we did."

Kirby stared at him, so shocked that he could not say or do anything except sit there motionless. Then Suzy squeezed his hand and said, "It's true, Kirby. There isn't any doubt about it."

TWELVE

KIRBY put his hand to his throbbing head. For a time his mind simply refused to function. He had spent many hours with Dave Thorn; they had talked about a multitude of subjects, but the man's interest in the South or secession or slavery had never come out. Kirby shook his head and turned his gaze to Kane.

"This right?" Kirby asked.

Kane nodded. "You think he's your friend and you don't believe it?"

"No, I don't." Kirby answered.

"Why?" Arch Bland shouted.

Kirby told them how it had been with him and Thorn, including their argument tonight. They thought about it a moment, then Jones said, "He's clever, more clever than me and Suzy. Me, anyway. You see, Kirby, I pretended to be something I wasn't in Kansas, so it was easy to keep doing it when I got out here. That's how I know quite a bit about the other side. I'm reasonably certain that Thorn brought his horse herd out here to mount a band of cavalry when the shooting starts."

"Oh, I don't think he—" Kirby stopped, realizing he was foolish to say what he thought because he didn't know enough about it to think intelligently. Dave Thorn knew where Kirby stood, but if these people were right, Kirby didn't know where Thorn stood. He said, "I guess my trouble is that to me Thorn just isn't a trick man."

"He's trick enough," Kane said. "I look for him to come out into the open one of these times, but only when he's ready, not a minute before."

"He has some problems, too," Jones said. "They have a lot to do with when he does come into the open. He's a man with principles. That's more than you can say for most of the Bummers who are thieves and robbers and murderers. I suppose some of them sincerely sympathize with the South, but I'm convinced that the majority of them actually want to provoke a fight because it will give them more chance to plunder. Well, Thorn doesn't want to deal with these men. I don't think he even wants to be on their side, but he's stuck with them."

"You were attacked out there on Cherry Creek, weren't you?" Kane asked.

Kirby nodded. "How did you know?"

"I told him," Jones said. "I heard about it in the Criterion a few hours after it happened. It's no secret why you're here or what you believe. Don't forget Sam Riley was killed the first night he was in Denver. He talked too much and too loud. The other side considers you far more dangerous than Riley, so some of them decided to rub you out before you got to Denver."

"They fired a few shots and rode on," Kirby said. "They must not have been very anxious to get me."

"They heard Mrs. Thorn scream," Jones said, "so they thought they had shot her and got panicky. Thorn was sore about it when he heard what had happened. He beat hell out of one of the men who told him. They didn't try it again. I guess they were afraid of him."

"Firing Kirby doesn't make sense," Suzy said. "We thought he gave Kirby a job so he could keep an eye on him and lead them to us. He wants to identify our spies as much as we want to identify his. I mean we thought he did."

"I still think he does," Kane said thoughtfully, "but maybe he lost his temper. If that's so, he's wishing he hadn't by now. When you see him again, he may offer you your job back."

"Do I take it?"

Kane shook his head. "No. I'm getting to that, but first I want to give you the explanation you asked for. As you know, I've tailed you almost every night since you got to

Denver. We have a job for you, and I wanted to see how you actually performed in a crowd. If you drank too much . . . if you gambled too much . . . or if you talked too much, we didn't want you and I would not have made the contact, but I was impressed by the way you handled yourself." He laughed softly. "And by the way you handled me, although you should have been tougher than you were. You were too gullible. You believed me when you shouldn't have."

Kirby thought of what they'd said about Dave Thorn and decided it was true. "I won't argue on that point," he said. "I was wondering why I didn't hear from any of you. I didn't have much to go on, you know. Montgomery said someone would get in touch with me."

"We heard about you through Arch, who got word from Montgomery," Kane went on. "I had my own connections with Bill and his sister. There are several more men who belong to this chapter, but I thought it was better if you didn't know all of them and they didn't all know you."

Kirby considered this. It made him uneasy, for he had the feeling he was still on trial. He said, "I don't know why I shouldn't know them and they shouldn't know me."

"I'll tell you," Kane said. "When you walk out of this cabin you're on your own. If you get into trouble, you work your way out or you're dead. We may change our policy later, but as it stands now, you are not to recognize any of us if you see us on the street. The fewer of us you know, the less chance there is that you'll give any of us away."

Kirby's jaw set. "I aim to see Suzy."

Kane did not smile. "No harm in that. They can't make anything out of it, seeing as you were interested in her before, but remember you had a fight with Bill. Outside of this cabin you are not his friend. You report to me. No one else. If anyone sees you coming here or leaving and wonders about it, tell them I'm grubstaking you. I have several prospectors in the mountains now that I grub-staked, so they'll believe you."

"I'll remember," Kirby said.

"You will move to the Broadwell House tomorrow," Kane went on. "You will live there until after the election. If Lincoln wins, we'll have a war. I'm sure of it, although there aren't many here who agree with me."

"I do," Arch Bland said.

"So does Montgomery," Kirby said.

"Then I don't stand alone." Kane smiled briefly as he handed Kirby a folded piece of paper. "As soon as you hear that Lincoln is elected, if he is, you will start for Boulder, then go to Gold Hill, Golden City, Black Hawk, and the other camps around there. I'm giving you the names of our brothers to see in each camp. I want to know how many men can be depended on if it comes to a fight. If anyone knows, our brothers you are seeing will. Take your time because you'll hit snow and cold weather. I don't look for any real trouble until spring, or at least not until after Lincoln's inauguration, but of course we can't be sure in this kind of game."

Kirby looked at the men seated at the table, then at Suzy, who was watching him intently. He said, "All right, I'll do my best."

"Now I suggest you take Suzy home," Kane said, his gaze pinned again on the girl. "If Thorn asks where you were, tell him you were with Suzy."

She rose, winking at Kirby. "I thought I never was going to get you to myself."

Kirby stood up, uncertain about his position in the organization, but he would hear nothing more from any of them now. His dismissal was plain enough. He said, "Good night," and, opening the door, followed Suzy into the darkness.

THIRTEEN

SUZY turned left when she and Kirby reached Fifth Street. He asked, "Where do you and Bill live?"

"A couple of blocks from here," she said. "The corner of Fifth and Ferry. Mr. Kane had rented the cabin for us, so it was ready to move into when we got here. We were lucky. Good cabins are hard to find."

He was silent for a block, thinking about the meeting he had just left, and about Dave and Liz Thorn. He had not known what to expect when he'd gone to Martin Kane's cabin, but he certainly never had dreamed he would run into Suzy and Bill Jones, and he had been almost as surprised to hear that Dave Thorn was a leader of the proslavery faction.

"How did they happen to let you into the Brotherhood?" he asked. "As far as I know there are no women members in Kansas."

"I'm not really a member," she said. "When they have a chapter meeting, they don't let me in, but it was a little different tonight because you were coming. I'm a spy the same as Bill. I run a bakery business and take orders and deliver bread and such to the . . . the women of ill repute. When I'm in their places, I listen. You'd be surprised what I learn just by appearing young and innocent and keeping my ears open." She laughed. "I guess I haven't been any great help to Martin Kane though."

"I hope I will." He paused, then added, "Looks like I was pretty well tested before they let me in. I'm not sure Kane completely trusts me yet."

"He tested you, all right," she said. "After all, you had a reputation of being a radical back in Kansas. Anyone who was associated with Montgomery's Jayhawkers had that reputation, and you sort of inherited your father's, which made it worse. When Sam Riley got to Denver, he turned out to be the worst kind of a fool, so Martin Kane wanted to make sure you wouldn't act the same way."

"Yes, I heard about Sam getting shot in the Criterion."

"Well, he shouldn't have gone there in the first place because he knew it was the center of the secesh crowd. Then after he got there he kept on drinking until he was roaring drunk, and he was so obnoxious nobody could stand him. He told the crowd he was going to see that the slavery people were run out of the country and you were going to help him."

"He named me?" Kirby asked incredulously.

"He certainly did," she said. "Bill was there and heard him. He didn't try to save Riley's life. He couldn't have in the first place, and in the second place Bill didn't think it was worth saving. Anyhow, Riley brought his death on himself. What's more, Bill thinks he was responsible for the raid that was made on your camp. He also thinks you would be dead by now if Dave Thorn hadn't passed the word to let you alone. We don't know what his motives were, but he probably liked you well enough to want you to stay alive, or he thought you would lead him to us."

"I guess they all know who I am by now," Kirby said sourly. "Funny they haven't followed me around like Kane did."

She had her hand in his and now she squeezed it. "They did, darling. They used several men, none of them often enough so you would recognize them. Kane knew you'd catch on if he was the only one on our side who tailed you. I think he wanted you to so he could see what you'd do before he made contact. After you jumped him, he talked to Bill and Randy Curl and decided to bring you into the Brotherhood."

"Thorn's men may have followed me to Kane's cabin," Kirby said.

"I doubt that it makes any difference," she said. "Bill is the only one who was there tonight that they think is on their side, and he won't leave the cabin until Kane and Curl have made sure the coast is clear."

They had reached her cabin, and she paused for a moment, facing him. In the darkness all he could see was a pale oval; he could not make out her expression, but he heard her breathing and felt her hands on his arms and suddenly he knew he had to go, that he could not risk getting involved with Suzy any more than he was. If Bill and Suzy and the rest of them were right about Dave Thorn, he might kill Kirby the instant he stepped through the door of his cabin.

He started to back away, but she would have none of it. She slipped her arms around him, saying softly, "Kirby, I know I'm a brazen woman, but I'm not one bit ashamed. I don't mind telling you that I've just about gone crazy worrying over you. I wanted to go to your camp on Cherry Creek and warn you when I heard about the raid, but Bill wouldn't let me. Even after you got to Denver I wanted to warn you so at least you'd know what to expect from Thorn, but Bill wouldn't let me do that either. Kane is the boss, and he didn't want you told anything until he was ready to contact you."

"With Kane feeling the way he does," Kirby said, "I guess it was a good thing you didn't say anything to me the night I had the fight with Bill."

"I guess so," she admitted, "although at the time there wasn't anything I could tell you except that we were on your side and to take it easy when Bill jumped you. He wanted Thorn and the other proslavery people to think he believed the way they did. At least they'd assume you and Bill were enemies after you'd had the fight."

"I don't know whether I'd have believed you if you had told me," Kirby said thoughtfully, "although you did say that people were not always what they seemed. I guess I should have caught on then."

She was silent for a moment, then she said, "I was so glad you told Martin Kane you aimed to see me. We'll have to be careful, though. Kane wants you to come here only after dark, when Bill will be gone. If Thorn keeps a man on you, he might wonder why you and Bill are suddenly acting friendly."

He was only half listening. A moment before he had felt impelled to leave before he was involved any more than he was, but now, just as suddenly, he remembered how alone and friendless he had felt. He had no reason to feel that way now. Suzy had told him as boldly as a woman could that she loved him.

He pulled her to him and kissed her. The instant their lips met, she became a flame in his arms. Brazen or bold or unashamed made no difference to him. He loved her and he needed her, and the problems and intrigues that offered so many pitfalls for him became unimportant. Her breasts pressing against his chest were so soft, her lips so sweet that for this moment nothing was important except that he loved her and he was no longer alone and unloved.

When their lips parted, he said, "I love you, Suzy. I didn't want to say it yet. I thought it would be better if we waited until the trouble was over."

"Why, we might wait for years!" she cried. "Let's not wait at all. Let's get married tomorrow."

He wondered what Martin Kane would say, or if it made any difference to him. And her brother Bill. "I'd like to," he said. "I'm as crazy as you are. I feel as if I've been caught in a strong current and I don't have any choice about what I do. I want you, Suzy. That's all I can think of."

"It's all I've thought about for quite a while," she said. "You'll find a preacher tomorrow?"

He took a long breath, his natural caution coming back to him. He said, "Ask Bill. And your friend Kane. It's like you said. He's the boss. If he thinks our getting married will interfere—"

"Oh, damn," she said. "Of course he'll say it will inter-fere. We're soldiers fighting a war, and he's our general. Kirby, I've heard it a dozen times. I . . . I guess he's right."

"I guess he is." Kirby kissed her again, lightly this time. Disappointed, he started to turn away, then stopped. "Suzy, what did Laurie and Duke do?"

"They left town. That's all I know." She gripped his arms. "I don't know, Kirby. I really don't. I love you so much, and sometimes I get kind of sick and empty in the pit of my stomach when I think I'll never have you. Laurie is little and pathetic and she needs you, but I'm just a redheaded blob of temper. I don't have to have anybody. I can always take care of myself."

"You're jealous," he said incredulously. "But she's married, Suzy."

"Yes," she said. "I know I'm crazy, but I am jealous. I just can't help it."

"I said she was married."

"But not because she loves Duke," Suzy said, "and he certainly doesn't love her. After Sam was shot, she was as helpless as a child. She clung to him so hard I guess he couldn't do anything but marry her. He was broke, you know. He lost everything except his team and wagon the first night in the Elephant Corral, so he mar-ried Laurie and sold her outfit and left town."

"That's about the way I thought it would go," he said.

He was tired. Too much had happened tonight. He had warned Laurie, but she had refused to believe him. No, he wasn't in love with her. He was just sorry for her.

"I'll see you tomorrow night," he said. "Just remember

90

I love you, not another man's wife."

He wheeled and strode away into the darkness. He was committed and he was glad. She had all the fire and passion that a man could want in a woman. Still, looking back, he wasn't sure how it had happened. But maybe a man never did. He had heard it said that these things were always managed by the women, and if he asked Suzy, she would say of course she had managed it.

For a moment his mind turned to Martin Kane. He was, Kirby thought, the most puzzling human being he had ever met. He said the right words, but as Kirby thought about what had happened in the Kane cabin, it seemed to him there was a falseness about the man. He could not identify it exactly, but he had a feeling that while Kane was saying one thing, he had been thinking quite another.

Then Kirby remembered how often Kane's eyes had been pinned on Suzy's face. The possibility that Kane was in love with her occurred to him, but he dismissed the thought as preposterous. Kane was a cold man if he'd ever seen one, not the type to care for any woman—certainly not a fiery redhead. Kirby, my boy, he said to himself, you're as jealous as Suzy, and not near as smart.

FOURTEEN

KIRBY had never been serious about a girl before, and he'd had no intention of getting serious with Suzy. Now, having taken a roundabout way back to Thorn's because he wanted to think about his situation, he tried to consider it calmly.

The sober truth was that Suzy would be hard to live with. She actually seemed proud of her temper, but to him it was not something in which she should take pride. He found himself comparing her to Laurie because she had done it. Laurie might not be as exciting as Suzy, but she did need someone to take care of her, and she was always very grateful for any favor that was done for her.

He dismissed the subject from his mind. Laurie was married for better or worse, and he was not a man to disrupt a marriage. Still, the knowledge was in him that if he found Duke Rome abusing Laurie, he'd kill the man. He had never felt that way about anyone else, and he wondered if he was in love with Laurie and didn't know it, if Suzy had sensed this. No, he was in love with Suzy whether he wanted to be or not, and sometimes the hunger for her was so great he thought he could not bear it. But that was not enough for a successful marriage. If Laurie had not married. . . . But it had not occurred to him to court her when she was free. . . .

The Thorn cabin was directly ahead of him when the thought came to him that no matter how hard he tried to keep Laurie out of his mind, she had a way of creeping back in.

Usually Dave and Liz Thorn went to bed early and got up early, but both were sitting by the stove drinking coffee when he went in. He was not prepared for this meeting, and when he saw Thorn look at him and frown, he knew he would not take anything from the man. A wave of anger swept through him. He hated Dave Thorn because he had once admired and respected him; he had thought they were friends, but now he knew that Thorn had tricked him from the beginning, and had taken advantage of his friendship and respect.

He stood just inside the door, his fists clenched at his sides as he met Thorn's gaze. Liz said, "Won't you have a cup of coffee before you go to bed?"

"No thanks," Kirby answered, his gaze not wavering from Thorn's face. "Is it all right for me to sleep here tonight? I told you I'd move out in the morning."

"Sure it's all right." Thorn's gaze wavered then and he set his cup on the table and reached for his pipe and tobacco. "I wanted to talk to you about that. That's why we stayed up. It ain't easy for me to apologize to anyone, even Liz, but I'm apologizing to you, Kirby. I'm sorry I lost my temper."

"It's all right, Dave," Kirby said, relieved by the knowledge that Thorn was not going to push the issue. Old loyalties died hard in him, and even though he could hate Thorn for deceiving him, he still did not want to fight with him. "I'll move out in the morning like I said, and you can find a man who will obey your orders without giving you an argument."

"I said I was sorry," Thorn snapped. "I want you to keep your job and go on living here with us. Jobs are hard to find and will be until spring. Room and meals are expensive. Liz wants you . . . we both like to have you living here with us."

Kirby shook his head. "I didn't intend to work for you, Dave. I still don't know why I said I would. I figured I'd just look around this winter and keep my eyes open. By spring I thought I'd hear of something I wanted."

"God damn it!" Thorn shouted. "Does a man have to get down on his knees to you? I'm sorry I asked you to take the shift at the barn. I'm sorry I didn't ask you sooner so you could have made other arrangements about your date. I'm sorry I got sore and told you that you'd have to take my orders if you wanted to keep your job." His face had turned red and he began to tremble with rage. "Now is that enough?"

Kirby glanced at Liz. She was plainly worried as she watched her husband. He brought his gaze back to Thorn, who was gripping the tabletop so hard his knuckles were white. There was more to this than was apparent, Kirby thought. Martin Kane had been right. Thorn was sorry he had lost his temper, and he was offering Kirby's job back to him. He was not a man to grovel, and only an extreme situation would make him do it.

"No, Dave," Kirby said gently. "I made other arrangements tonight. I'll be leaving Denver before long."

He walked past the table and climbed the ladder to his attic room. He lighted a candle and took off his clothes, wondering if he should have told Thorn he knew all about him. Deciding that would have been wrong, he blew out the candle and went to bed. It was just as well that Thorn went on thinking that Kirby did not know. Perhaps he had no idea that the Union men were aware of the role he was playing.

Kirby lay staring into the darkness, remembering that Liz had acted as if she were disappointed when he had told her he was going to work for them. He liked her, and he was sure she liked him. Thorn was tough enough to decree another man's death if it seemed necessary for the defense of the cause he was supporting, but Kirby didn't think Liz was. Possibly she was afraid for his life and thought he would be safer if he had no connection with Dave. If he had an opportunity, he would ask her.

He slept later than usual Sunday morning. When he went downstairs he found that Thorn was gone. Liz said, "Good morning, Kirby. I'll fix your breakfast right away. I'll pour a cup of coffee, and you can drink it while you're waiting."

He sat down at the table and drank the coffee she brought to him. She started bacon frying, then glanced over her shoulder. "You didn't change your mind about going back to work for Dave?"

"No," he answered. "I can't. I told you I'd be leaving Denver before long."

She turned the bacon, then came to the table and sat down across from him. She asked softly, "You know, don't you? You found out last night."

He was not entirely surprised that she had sensed his knowledge of the part her husband was playing, but he hadn't thought it would come out so soon and so clearly, and he doubted that Dave knew she was saying it. He studied her a moment before he answered, "That's right. Are you going to tell Dave that I know?"

She shook her head. "I don't think so. I didn't approve of him asking you to go to work for him in the first place. You've been open and aboveboard in letting everyone know how you felt. I thought Dave should have been equally honest with you. And I was afraid that something might happen that would make it necessary for them to kill you. They would, you know. McCoy was a Border Ruffian as you jayhawkers call some of us, and he's done his share of killing."

She returned to the stove. A short time later she brought his breakfast to him and sat down again. "Dave thinks a great deal of you, Kirby. He's sorry that the necessities of war put you on opposite sides. It is war. You realize that as fully as we do." She lowered her head so he could not see her eyes. "I've told you that I wanted a son like you. I hope you won't be hurt by what happens. Or by anything that Dave does."

"I guess we'll all be taking chances." Then, to change the subject, he told her he had seen Suzy the night before. "We'll get married as soon as we can," he finished.

"I'm glad," she said, smiling. "Suzy is a fine girl."

Later, after he had packed his suitcase and was ready to leave, she said, "Think well of us if you can, Kirby."

He set his suitcase down and put his arms around her. He said, "I can always think well of you, Liz."

She looked up at him, blinking. She whispered, "Try to think well of Dave, too, Kirby. He's a man who's driven by something. I'm not always sure what it is. At times he seems to be pulled one way and then the other." She swallowed, and added, "You don't know about it, Kirby, but if it hadn't been for Dave, you'd be dead by now."

"I won't forget," he said.

Picking up his suitcase, he left the cabin. He went directly to the Broadwell House and took a room, then he walked to Thorn's barn. McCoy eyed him malevolently but did not say a word all the time that it took

Kirby to saddle his buckskin. Thorn wasn't in sight and Kirby didn't ask McCoy about him. It was a good thing, he thought, that Thorn was gone.

Kirby rode to the Elephant Corral, left the buckskin there, and returned to the Broadwell House, certain he was followed. This man, he was sure, was one of Thorn's. Apparently he had not been followed last night. Perhaps Thorn had not had a man available. That could explain why he had tried so hard to keep Kirby where he could watch him. One thing was sure. He was still trying to use Kirby to identify Martin Kane and his associates.

FIFTEEN

DURING the next few weeks Kirby occasionally saw Martin Kane, Randy Curl, and Bill Jones on the street or in a saloon. He never gave a sign of recognition to the first two and neither did they; he and Bill would nod stiffly at each other. Kirby did not see Archibald Bland and he wondered about that, finally deciding that Kane and the others had sent him out of town. Like Sam Riley, Bland might talk too much. Kirby had judged him to be that kind of man.

Kirby saw Suzy every night, but he was always careful to wait until after dark before going to the Jones cabin so he could be sure that Bill was gone. It did not seem important whether he ran into Bill or not, but apparently it was to Martin Kane, so Kirby obeyed the order. Suzy did not mention Laurie. Kirby didn't either. He was satisfied to keep his relationship with Suzy as pleasant as possible, and it was very pleasant indeed.

He had a haunting feeling that he was living in a calm between storms. On November 13 the Jefferson Territorial Provisional Legislature met at Apollo Hall to form a temporary organization, then it adjourned as soon as officers were elected, to convene again the following day to hear Governor Steele's annual message. Almost as soon as the delegates were in the street, a Pony Express rider brought the news that Lincoln had been elected.

Kirby was in the post office when a man rushed in shouting, "Old Abe got hisself elected." Park McClure, the postmaster, who was one of the most outspoken proslavery men in town, cursed as if he were a wild man and bellowed that blood would flow like a river if Lincoln tried to free the slaves.

Although darkness was hours away, Kirby broke Kane's rule and went to the Jones cabin to give Suzy the news. He found her baking cakes to fill an order from Ada LaMont's house. She was wearing a blue-and-white-checked apron, and Kirby, stopping just inside the door to stare at her, thought she was even more attractive than usual.

She raised a hand to her face to scratch her nose, leaving a dab of flour there when she dropped her hand to the table. She asked, "What was all the yelling about?"

"You're the prettiest girl I ever saw," Kirby told her. "I'm struck dumb every time I look at you and see how beautiful you are."

"Oh, go on now," she said, pleased. "I declare, Kirby. You claim you're not Irish, but you must have kissed the

Blarney Stone the way you talk."

"Bill here?"

"No. He went to the Criterion."

"Good." Kirby crossed the room to her and took her into his arms. "Then I can kiss you good and proper as soon as I tell you that Lincoln was elected."

She was not surprised. She said, "Well, we knew he would be, didn't we?"

"Douglas could have got it," Kirby said. "I guess there were as many men in town betting on him as there were on Old Abe."

"Now about the kissing you mentioned," Suzy said. "It sounds more interesting than politics. Besides, I've got to get these cakes baked."

He kissed her, good and proper as he had promised. When she drew back from him, she began to smooth her red hair. "I should never allow you to do that," she told him. "I think that every time, but I forget."

"I don't know why," he said. "I like it."

"Oh, I like it, all right." She gave him a saucy grin and turned back to the table. "That's the whole trouble. You get along now. I've got work to do."

"I'll be back tonight," he said. "I look for everybody with Republican sympathies to get together for a celebration. I thought it would be all right for me to take you."

"I guess Kane would allow it," she said with a trace of bitterness in her voice. "Go on now. You'll have me so unstrung that I'll put salt instead of sugar in these cakes."

"I can sit over here and just watch you."

"No, you won't do any such thing. Just being here in the room does things to me. It gets my mind off my business onto . . . onto other things."

He still hesitated, knowing that he would be leaving for Boulder in the morning and he had no idea when he would see her again. Maybe never, for he realized he was a marked man. He was being followed almost every night, and he wondered if he could get out of town in the morning without having a man ride behind him.

He glanced around the big room with the cookstove and table and shelves filled with sacks and cans of food. Bill's bed, which was covered by a white lace spread, was against the wall on the other side of the room. A curtain enclosed the corner behind it. Suzy's bed was there. It gave her little privacy, but it was better than nothing, she had told Kirby, and added that he'd better hurry up and marry her so she could have her own home.

"I'll be back about dark," he said abruptly and, wheeling, strode out of the cabin and back along Fifth Street, crossed the Cherry Creek bridge and went on to the Broadwell House.

He had thought a great deal about Martin Kane since the night of the meeting. He had not gone back to see the man because there had been nothing to report, and his orders had been definite. Now that he knew he would be riding out of Denver early in the morning, he wished he had called on Kane again. He should know the man better than he did. Some men, like Archibald Bland and even Bill Jones, were not difficult to understand. Now that he knew about Dave Thorn, he could look back and realize that some of Thorn's actions which were puzzling at the time were no longer puzzling.

But the more he thought about Kane, the more of an enigma he seemed. When he first noticed Kane turning up in saloons a minute or so after he did, he had thought of him as a man who would never stand out in a crowd. Then as soon as Kirby was inside the cabin with Kane, he had known that this was a sort of disguise, that Martin Kane was a strong individual who gave orders that would be obeyed. Oh, he had been pleasant and friendly enough, but the more Kirby thought about that evening, the more he realized that Kane had completely over-shadowed everyone else there.

Kirby had known almost at once that Archibald Bland was a fanatic, but now, thinking back, he wondered if Martin Kane wasn't a fanatic, too. He did not show it by what he said or by anything he had done thus far, but he was a coldblooded machine, a man who would unhesi-tatingly carry out any execution order if he were the one delegated to do it.

Kirby called for Suzy a few minutes before seven. The evening was cold and she wore a heavy coat. She took his arm as they moved toward the corner of Larimer and G streets. Neither said a word until they were in front of the Wallingford and Murphy store which was less than half a block from where the crowd was gathering.

"Kirby," Suzy said.

"What?"

"Bill was home about six," she said. "He told me that McClure and Charley Harrison and the rest of the Southern sympathizers are so furious over Lincoln's election that they think war is a certainty."

"That's one place where I can agree with them," he said.

"I've got something to tell you," she said, "but it will wait until we get back."

They stood near the edge of the crowd as General Larimer, one of the town fathers, called the meeting to order. About three hundred people were massed in the intersection of the two streets, Kirby judged. First a hundred-gun salute was fired to honor the election of the Republican candidate. The crowd had circled a huge fire which was burning in the street. Three or four cords of wood had been hauled here before dark and now men were throwing it on the fire until it blazed high and threw out so much heat that those nearest to the flames were forced to retreat.

Kirby and Suzy listened to the cheers for Lincoln and several patriotic songs and speeches until Suzy tugged at his arm and said, "Let's go back. Bill's staying all night at the Criterion. He thinks there'll be some plans made tonight by the secesh crowd."

They walked back to her cabin, her hand clutching his arm. When they were inside and out of the cold, Suzy locked the door and built up the fire. She put the coffeepot on the stove, then disappeared behind her curtain. She returned in a moment wearing a blue robe which was tightly bound around her waist by a cord.

"I hope you won't mind me being comfortable," she said. He nodded approvingly as he looked at her. He had never seen her quite like this before. She was not the bold and brazen women she tried to pretend she was. For this moment at least she seemed almost timid. She glanced at him questioningly and then looked away as if wanting his approval more than anything else in the world.

"I don't mind at all," he said.

She brought cups and plates and silverware to the table, poured the coffee and then uncovered a chocolate cake that was on the table. She said, "I kept this one back. Ada didn't like it because I was one short, but I lied and told her I just couldn't get them all baked today. I'll see that she gets the extra one tomorrow."

She cut a piece, lifted it to a plate and passed it to him. He said, "You had something to tell me."

"I've got two things," she said, "but first I'd better tell you I want you to stay with me tonight. I'm frightened. There are so many drunks who—" She paused, then hurried on, "With Bill gone, I don't want to stay alone." She glanced at him and laughed. "I suppose I'm not fooling you one bit, but I am scared."

"I'll stay as long as you want me," he said.

She showed her relief. She started to cut a piece of cake for herself, then stopped and laid the knife down. Her hand was trembling so much she couldn't control it. After a time she said, "I'm going to make a confession, and I hope you will still love me. Sometimes I think I lie more than I tell the truth. I lied about Laurie because I was jealous and I'm ashamed. I know where they are. They're in Gold Hill and you're going there after you leave Boulder. I'm sure you'll find them." She reached out and laid a hand over his. "Am I forgiven?"

"Of course," he said.

"I'm glad." She picked up the knife and this time succeeded in cutting a piece of cake and lifting it to her plate. "The other thing I haven't told you is about Martin Kane. I don't know how the Brotherhood worked in Kansas, but here Kane is a dictator. He fancies himself a general, he says we're in his army, and we wouldn't have enlisted in it unless we are dedicated to the proposition of making this a free state."

"That's about the way I sized him up," Kirby said.

"You still don't understand that you risk your life by working for the Brotherhood," Suzy said. "If you don't succeed in doing what you were told to do, and Kane thinks you haven't tried hard enough, or that you're sorry of your bargain and you're about to make a run for it, or even that you might call too much attention to yourself and the organization and give away some of their secrets, he'll have you killed."

Kirby put his fork down and looked at her. What she had said reminded him of his conversation with Dave Thorn when they were camped on Cherry Creek and Thorn had just returned from Denver. Thorn had told him about the Vigilantes, ten men who take you out and hang you if they have decided that is to be your fate. You don't have a public trial, you have no right to defend yourself, and you don't have a lawyer. If Suzy was right, the Vigilantes operated exactly the way Martin Kane did.

"Do you think Kane is the head of the Vigilantes?" Kirby asked. "Or that he belongs to the inner ten?"

"I don't know," she answered. "Neither does Bill, but sometimes I know he's scared that Kane will decide he has to be killed. Oh, he doesn't say so, but I know him so well that I can tell. He's between two fires, you see.

If the secesh crowd gets onto him, they'll kill him. If Kane suspects him of disloyalty, or of failure, the Brotherhood will kill him."

Kirby finished his cake and picked up his cup of coffee. Somehow it seemed as if he were being given a preview of a nightmare. He shook his head, unable to accept this as being real. "Whatever Kane is," Kirby said, "he's not stupid. I can't believe he'd have me or Bill killed because of a suspicion. He can't afford to lose people like us."

"No, he can't," she agreed, "but he claims he can't afford to take the risk of letting the enemy know about him and the Brotherhood and their plans." She had been nibbling at her cake. Now she pushed the plate back. "Do you have any idea what happened to Archibald Bland?"

"I hadn't seen him around town," Kirby said. "I thought that maybe Kane had told him to leave. Bland was the impatient kind. He could be the sort of man you were talking—" He stared at her, a little sick as he realized what she was suggesting. "You aren't trying to tell me they killed him?"

She nodded. "You'll remember Kane dismissed us suddenly. There were two purposes in holding the meeting that night. One was to talk to you. The other was to try Bland because he had been talking too much. He planned to ask a member of the territorial legislature to introduce a measure forbidding slavery in Jefferson Territory. He bragged that he and his friends were going to run all the proslavery men out of the country. Bill, Kane and Randy Curl tried him that night and convicted him. Kane took him up Clear Creek and killed and buried him."

Kirby rose and walked to the stove. He stood there, his hands jammed into his pockets. To believe in something, to be willing to fight and die for it if necessary was one thing; to be suspected and condemned to death for that suspicion was quite another thing.

"Had Bland been warned?" he asked.

She nodded. "Maybe they were right. Bill swears they were. They couldn't shut Bland up any more than they could shut Sam Riley up. Of course Sam was a fool and Bland wasn't, but the danger was basically the same. Bland seemed to think he was another John Brown. Maybe he was just as crazy as Brown. But even if they were right to kill Bland, they might be wrong the next time."

He stood beside the stove thinking about it. This was a question of expediency. He had argued it with his father and Colonel Montgomery many times. How far did you go against your conscience in little matters in order to win the big one? How far did the end justify the means?

No one had an answer, but it seemed queer to Kirby that a man like Martin Kane considered Bland and Colonel Montgomery dangerous men just as he would have considered John Brown dangerous. At the same time Kirby knew that his father and Montgomery would have considered Kane dangerous if they were here to pass judgment on him.

Was it right to do anything, to commit any crime, to keep the Union together and make Jefferson Territory a free state? Or was it wrong for three men to take upon themselves the authority to pass a death sentence on a man and carry it out because they considered him a weak link in their chain?

He shook his head. "You're right, Suzy," he said. "They might be wrong the next time."

She rose and came to him. She put her arms around him and laid her head against his chest. "Darling, that's why I'm frightened. For you, not myself. You're leaving in the morning on a mission that is more dangerous than you ever dreamed of it being. I may never see you again. I want you for my husband even if it is only for tonight. I couldn't stand it if I never had you at all."

He put his arms around her and said softly, "It will be for more than tonight. I promise you."

But afterwards he wasn't so sure. He remembered how Martin Kane's gaze had returned to Suzy time after time that evening when they had been in Kane's cabin. If the man were in love with Suzy, he would have his own reason for disposing of a rival and still have the excuse of doing it in the name of the cause in which they both believed. Now, quite suddenly, the idea did not seem preposterous at all.

SIXTEEN

KIRBY left Denver in the cold darkness of early morning. He followed the Boulder road that ran north, glancing back now and then to see if he were being followed. Shortly after daybreak he saw that a horseman was behind him. At first he thought this did not prove anything. Certainly there could be men on the

Boulder road at this hour who knew nothing about Kirby Grant. That was what he wanted to believe. The truth was he didn't want to think that Martin Kane had sent a man to watch him, perhaps kill him, and he wanted even less to think that Dave Thorn had ordered him murdered.

The man stayed far enough behind so that Kirby was unable to tell anything about him. When Kirby slowed up, the man behind slowed, and when Kirby touched up his horse, the man behind increased his speed so that the distance between them remained the same.

Shortly after twelve the road turned west toward the mountains. Kirby buttoned his coat collar around his neck and pulled his black felt hat low over his eyes. He was riding into the wind now; it had a sharp bite to it, and the clouds had dropped so low that the foothills of the Rockies which rose directly from the plains were hidden from sight.

The man stayed behind, skillfully keeping the same distance between them. At times the black clouds made the light so thin that the fellow disappeared, but Kirby soon saw him again, a vague, ghostly figure that sent prickles of fear skittering along Kirby's spine. It wouldn't be so bad, he thought, if he knew for sure what the man's intentions were.

Kirby considered turning around and asking him point blank. He laughed at himself, knowing that the man would lie if he intended to kill him. No, the only thing he could do was to go on.

Kirby came to a ranch and turned into the yard. A man stepped out of the house, calling above the wind, "You want dinner?"

"That's right," Kirby shouted back.

The rancher jerked his thumb toward the log shed back of the house. "Put your horse up and come in. Dinner's ready."

Kirby rode to the shed, dismounted, and opened the door. He led his horse inside, tied him in a stall and loosened the cinch. His gun belt was fastened outside his heavy coat. He pulled his glove from his right hand, lifted the revolver from the holster and checked it, then eased it back into the leather.

When Kirby stepped outside, he expected the man who had been following him to be waiting, but no one was in sight. He closed the shed door and hurried to the house. As he turned the corner, he saw that the rider was still in the road, perhaps fifty yards away. He was obviously waiting for Kirby to go into the house before he came any closer. For a moment Kirby hesitated, again tempted to face the man and have it out with him.

Kirby turned to the door, knowing that nothing had changed. He still had to play it out. He went inside, feeling the pleasant warmth of the room as he closed the door. He stripped the glove from his left hand and took off his hat.

"Hang your hat and coat there by the door," the rancher said. "That wind is a sonuvagun, now ain't it?"

"Sure is," Kirby agreed, rubbing his face with his hands. "How far is Boulder?"

"Seven, eight miles," the rancher said. "You picked a bad day for a ride."

"That I did," Kirby agreed.

He removed his gun belt, took off his coat and hung it

up, then quickly buckled his belt around his waist. He moved to a window in time to see the man who had been behind him turn into the yard from the road.

"Looks like you've got more business," Kirby said.

The rancher glanced outside, nodded, and opened the door wide enough to poke his head and yell for the rider to put his horse in the shed. He closed the door, saying, "We came here from Virginia last year, and damned if I've been warm since." He laughed as he held out his hand. "I'm Ira Beasley. I ain't as bad off as I let on, but I've been sick and I just can't seem to stand the cold no more."

"I'm Kirby Grant." Kirby shook hands, then walked to the fireplace and stood with his back to it. "How do you manage to get your chores done?"

"Oh, I've got a couple of boys who're in school right now," Beasley said. "They tend to things. We've got enough wood up for the winter and don't have much stock. Fact is, we do purty well feeding travelers like you." His wife came in from the kitchen with a platter of meat that she set on the table. "I'm lucky, Grant. My woman's a good rustler. My job is mostly fetching in the meat."

Mrs. Beasley laughed as she looked at Kirby. "Sure I'm a good rustler. So's Ira when I put the bee on him. We're about out of venison. He's gonna have to get out and fetch in a buck afore long."

Beasley groaned. "Oh hell, I thought this one was your turn."

"No siree." Mrs. Beasley winked at Kirby. "We're just like the Indians. He hunts and I cook. No hunt, no cook. That's fair enough, ain't it?"

"Sounds fair," Kirby agreed.

"Let's sit down," Beasley said as his wife disappeared into the kitchen again. "You know, if you're headed for the mines, you're making a mistake. We'll have snow on the ground afore night. Maybe won't get it down here, but back in the mountains where you'll be going there'll be too much to travel in."

Kirby walked around the table to stand with his back to the wall, his eyes on the door. He said, "Maybe I'll stay in Boulder."

Beasley took the bench at the head of the table as the door opened and the man came in. Beasley said, "Hang up your coat and hat and sit, mister. We're ready to eat."

The man turned his back to Kirby as he took off his hat and coat and hung them by the door, then he wheeled and strode to the table. Now, with his first close look at the man's face, Kirby was sure he didn't know him. He was about thirty, tall and very thin, with a saber of a nose and a pointed chin. He wore no beard, his hair and mustache were fiery red, and for a moment Kirby had a feeling that he was imagining trouble with the man. He was reasonably sure he would have remembered a face that was as distinctive as this one if he had seen him in Denver.

Beasley rose and held out his hand. "Ira Beasley," he said.

"John Deal," the tall man said as he shook hands, his thin lips curling into a quick grin that disappeared immediately.

"Pleased to meet you," Beasley said. "Help yourself to the biscuits, Deal, and pass 'em. That's honey yonder, and prune jam in the other dish. I sure do like my wife's biscuits." As Deal picked up the plate of biscuits and passed them, Beasley said, "I plumb forgot my manners. Our other guest is Kirby Grant. Grant, meet John Deal."

Deal shook hands with Kirby. He said, "I guess you've been ahead of me all morning, ain't you, Grant?"

Kirby nodded. "We seem to be traveling at about the same speed."

"I noticed that," Deal said, and began to eat.

Mrs. Beasley sat down at the other end of the table, her husband making no attempt to introduce Deal, who ate as if he were famished, his head lowered over his plate. Kirby ate slowly, his gaze on the man as the early suspicions returned to him.

Deal cleaned up his plate and lifted his head when he reached for a biscuit. For the first time Kirby noticed his eyes, pale blue that seemed to be entirely devoid of expression. Deal broke a biscuit, swiped it through the remains of gravy that was still on his plate and popped it into his mouth. He repeated the maneuver with the other half of the biscuit, then drank the rest of his coffee and rose.

"How much?" Deal asked.

"You ain't gonna leave without dessert, are you?" Mrs. Beasley demanded.

"I've got to get on to Boulder," Deal said. "How much?"

"Two dollars," Beasley said.

Deal dropped two silver dollars on the table, spun around and put on his coat and hat. He waited only long enough to buckle his gun belt around his coat, then went outside.

Beasley sighed in relief. "I'm glad to get rid of him. I'll admit I'm afraid of some of 'em that stop here. I was afraid of him."

Kirby nodded agreement. "He was behind me all the way from Denver. Now it looks like he's got reason to beat me into Boulder."

"You carrying any money?" Beasley asked.

"Not much."

"You'd best keep your eyes open anyway," Beasley said. "He's the kind who'd hold you up and kill you just for anything you had on you."

Kirby walked to a window and stood there until Deal rode away. The thought had been in Kirby's mind that Deal might wait in the shed and shoot him when he went in to get his horse. He had no doubt that John Deal, or whatever his name was, intended to kill him. He wasn't sure why he was so certain about it, but he'd had this feeling before when he had helped his father with runaway slaves on the underground railroad. He remembered that it was not a feeling to be ignored.

"I'll get your pie," Mrs. Beasley said.

Kirby shook his head as he returned to the table and laid two dollars on it. "I think I'd better go on," he said. "Thanks for the dinner."

"You're welcome," Mrs. Beasley said. "I hope you'll stop again sometime."

"I surely will if I ride by here at mealtime," Kirby said.

He put on his hat and coat, buckling his gun belt outside the coat. Beasley said, "You look like a man who can take care of himself, but just the same, you'd best watch out." He laughed nervously, and added, "When you meet all kinds like we do, you get so you can size 'em up purty good, but I had a different feeling about that man than I'd ever had before. When he went out, I had a crazy notion that something evil had left the house."

"It wasn't a crazy notion," Kirby said. "It was a fact."

He strode rapidly toward the shed, wondering if he were a fool to go on to Boulder today. Probably the Beasleys would put him up if he asked them to. Then he shrugged. It didn't make any difference. If Deal didn't get a chance to kill him today, he'd try tomorrow.

Kirby tightened the cinch, untied his buckskin, and led him out of the shed. He mounted and rode toward the mountains, his head tipped down so his face would not be exposed to the wind which carried light, swirling snowflakes. Now and then he glanced up, searching the country ahead of him, but he saw no one.

Uneasiness grew in him until he had to fight a panic that threatened to overpower him. If Deal was hiding in the brush along the side of the road, waiting to shoot him out of his saddle as he went by, there was nothing Kirby could do to defend himself unless Deal missed his first shot.

He reached Boulder late in the afternoon. Nothing had happened except that the snow had thickened so he could not see the buildings on the far side of the street distinctly. He had no way of knowing why Deal had not bushwhacked him, but he was thankful he was still alive.

Boulder was not much of a town, he thought. As he rode along the main street, he saw there were two or three stores, some saloons, and a collection of forty or more cabins and shacks strung out along Boulder Creek just below where it stormed down out of the mountains.

He found a livery stable and turned into it, not knowing whether Henry Elliot, the man he was to see, would have a place for him to leave his buckskin. He dismounted, gave directions for the care of the horse, and then asked where Elliot lived.

"Up the creek above town," the stableman said. "Just below the mouth of the canyon."

Kirby thanked him and turned toward the door. The snow filled the air so completely that the buildings across the street melted into one indistinct mass. As Kirby stepped through the door into the wind, the thought struck him with numbing impact that if this was the only livery stable in town, Deal would be reasonably sure of his coming here, and that would make this the perfect spot to cut him down.

Kirby yanked off his right-hand glove. Within the second a gun roared from across the street, the sound of it blasting into the whine of the wind like a great clap of thunder. The bullet slapped through the crown of Kirby's hat and buried itself in the log wall of the stable behind him.

He had his gun in his hand as he dived headlong into the snow, the second bullet missing by a good three feet. Lying on his belly, Kirby squeezed off two shots, aiming at the flash of powderflame he had seen through the falling snow. He rolled over and fired two more times, then he lunged to his feet and charged across the street.

He was nearly to the boardwalk on the other side before he realized that the dry gulcher was down, his face buried in the snow. The fingers of the man's outflung hands had dug into the frozen ground as he had tried desperately to drag himself to safety.

Kirby stood motionless as men drifted toward him. One of the first to arrive wore a star. He turned the dead man over and shook his head. "I never seen him around here. How about the rest of you?"

They said no. The man with the star turned to Kirby. "I reckon you'll admit you killed him. Got anything to say for yourself?"

"I sure have," Kirby said. "He tried to kill me. He threw a slug at me when I came out of the stable. He got off another before I hit the ground and started shooting."

"That's right," the stableman said. "I was looking at him when he went out of the barn. He hadn't touched his gun when I heard the first shot. You got no call to hold him, Marshal."

The lawman shrugged. "Guess I'll have to call it justifiable homicide. Got any idea why he tried to kill you?"

"No," Kirby said.

The marshal sighed. "That's the way it usually is. All right, boys. Pick him up and tote him over to Doc Updegraff's office."

Kirby walked away, thinking there was no use to tell the marshal that the man had eaten dinner with him a few hours ago at Beasley's place and had called himself John Deal. There was no use, either, to say that Dave Thorn or Martin Kane had sent John Deal to kill him. He had no proof whatever.

As he trudged through the snow, he decided it must have been Thorn. Kane was a paradoxical man who defied understanding, but he was coldly logical. It didn't make sense that he would order Kirby killed before he brought back his report. Later, perhaps, if he wanted a chance with Suzy and decided that there was only one way to get rid of his number one rival, but not now.

No, it had to be Thorn. The thought made Kirby sick. This kind of killing wasn't like Dave Thorn, not the Dave Thorn that Kirby Grant thought he knew.

SEVENTEEN

KIRBY walked upstream, wanting to get away from the crowd and the marshal in particular. He didn't want to be questioned about why he had come to Boulder.

Within five minutes he had left the town behind him. A moment later a cabin loomed up in the thin, snow-filtered light. He hoped this was Elliot's because he was getting chilled, probably as an aftermath of the shooting instead of the low temperature, he thought. It had shaken him, partly because he had not expected it in town and partly because he was alive on account of Deal's poor shooting, a miracle he could not hope to have happen again.

His knock on the cabin door brought a slatternly-looking woman who opened the door a crack. As she peered at him, he could see two runny-nosed children hanging onto her skirts. He backed away, the stench of dirty diapers insulting his nostrils.

"Is this Henry Elliot's place?" Kirby asked.

"Next place up the creek," the woman snapped, and slammed and locked the door.

He trudged on through the snow that was about two

inches deep now, first irritated and then amused. The woman was bragging on herself when she locked the door. Kirby felt certain that there was not a man in town would pay any attention to her. He had seen women in Denver who blatantly sold their charms who were cleaner, better dressed, and prettier by far than this one, yet he did not doubt that she considered herself a decent woman, superior in every way to the immoral women who were disgraces to the territory.

Through occasional breaks in the screen of willows along the creek he saw the swift water that was crystal clear as a mountain stream should be. Lacy edges of ice clung to both sides. At this time of year it was not a large stream, but he'd heard men talk about the spring runoff when the snow melted in the high country, turning small creeks into churning and often destructive torrents.

The thought crossed Kirby's mind that for all of man's digging in these mountains as he searched for gold, he would not make much difference with the creek, the canyon, or the mountains, all solid achievements of nature which would be here long after man had quit digging tunnels into the hillsides or working his arrastra wheels.

The storm had brought an early twilight by the time Kirby reached the next cabin. A tall man with a square-cut white beard opened the door to his knock and stood looking at him.

"You're Henry Elliot?" Kirby asked.

"That's right, friend," the bearded man said.

Kirby held out his hand. "I'm Kirby Grant," he said. "I rode out from Denver to see you."

Elliot offered his hand, and Kirby gave him the Brotherhood grip, his thumb pressing against the man's first knuckle, then moving to the second. Elliot returned the grip, his aloofness leaving him at once.

"Come in, Mr. Grant," Elliot said. "I have little to offer except a warm cabin. We're in for a cold night, I'm afraid. I don't have an extra bed and mine's not very comfortable, but I can fix a pallet on the floor for you. I was just cooking supper. You'll join me, won't you?"

"I'll be glad to," Kirby said as he stepped inside.

He stripped his gloves from his hands and slipped them into a coat pocket, then took off his hat and coat and hung them on a peg near the door. The interior of the cabin was neat and clean; the air was redolent with the smell of frying meat and boiling coffee and tobacco smoke. Quite a contrast, Kirby told himself, to the cabin where he had stopped a few minutes before.

He moved to the stove and held his hands out as he studied his host. In spite of his white beard, Elliot was not an old man; possibly fifty, but no more. He dropped another thick steak into his frying pan and glanced at Kirby, smiling.

"Got me a buck the other day," he said. "A three-point. Damned good eating. Beats the salt side you buy in town. Right now hunting's more profitable than prospecting. Looks like we might get a purty good snow out of this storm, so I reckon I'll be taking it easy unless Martin Kane thinks of something for me to do."

Kirby said nothing. He wasn't quite sure what Elliot was driving at, and he had the feeling that what he said might be repeated. Elliot set another place at the table and returned to the stove.

"Just offhand I'd say you was running an errand for Kane or you wouldn't be sashaying around in this kind of weather," Elliot said.

"You might say I am," Kirby admitted. "It damned near got me shot, too."

Elliot looked at him sharply. "Where did it happen?"

"In Boulder."

"Want to tell me about it?"

"Yeah, I sure do," Kirby said. "There's an angle I can't figure out."

Kirby began with his leaving Denver before daylight. When he finished, Elliot said, "Nothing hard to figure out in that. We've had men killed in this country before on account of the slavery question, or questions related to it. The secesh crowd in Denver certainly knows who you are, and sent Deal to smoke you down. It would make one less man to kill when the fighting starts, and it'll start one of these days. You mark my word."

"Sure it will," Kirby said impatiently, "but the angle I can't figure is why Deal waited till I got to town. He could have shot me without any danger to himself from a dozen places along the road."

Elliot turned to the stove and stared at the frying steaks. Then he said thoughtfully. "I think I know. There was always the chance that someone would spot him if he killed you on the road. He was probably smart enough to know the Beasleys would be suspicious if your body was found between their place and Boulder. What you don't know is that the Boulder marshal is friendly to the secesh crowd, so he probably knew Deal.

If the killing had gone the other way, as planned, he'd have called it justifiable homicide and Deal could have walked away, legally a free man."

Kirby nodded, thinking it made sense. He said, "That's probably it. Well, I guess now is as good a time as any to ask what I'm supposed to. Kane wants to know how the feeling is in Boulder, and how many men will really fight for the Union if it comes to that."

Elliot snorted. "Now that's a tall order and Martin knows it as well as I do. What I say is strictly a guess. You'd best remind him of it when you tell him."

"I don't think he expects you to take a poll," Kirby said.

Elliot grimaced. "He'd shoot me if I did."

Kirby glanced at him, wondering if he were being facetious when he said that, and decided he wasn't. "You mean he don't want us attracting attention?"

"That's it," Elliot said. "Talk's cheap, and it don't buy you nothing but trouble. I reckon you're the only one in this town who knows how I think. I spend most of my evenings in one of the saloons, and I listen to 'em gab. Some of it's drunken boasting about what they'll do if Lincoln gets elected."

"He was," Kirby said.

"Well, by grab, I'm glad to hear it," Elliot said, as if relieved. "After Old Abe's inaugurated next March, we'll see a thing or two. I don't reckon he'll free the slaves, but I don't figure he'll let the South pull out of the Union, neither."

Elliot took a pan of biscuits from the oven, and set them on the table, then poured the coffee and forked the meat into the tin plates. He said, "There's some cold beans yonder, and you'll find honey for your biscuits in that covered dish. Figure you can make out?"

"Sure can," Kirby said, as he sat down. "Now how about you answering my questions."

"I've been thinking," Elliot said. "Sort of counting noses of the men I can remember. We've got some boys here from way down South, and a few of 'em are regular Barnburners. Fact is, we've had a few knives pulled and some bloodletting on the subject, though most of the blood was more whiskey than blood."

He waggled a forefinger at Kirby. "The one thing I don't savvy is that some of the Southern sympathizers are Northern men who probably never saw a slave, but they've got a hell of a lot to say about States' rights. You can't really tell about a man like that, though I don't reckon they're likely gonna do much fighting for the South."

"Aren't there any Northern sympathizers?" Kirby asked.

"Sure." Elliot grinned. "Some of 'em are Barnburners like the Georgia boys. To hear a few of 'em talk, you'd think they had personally sent half the slaves in the South to Canada on the underground railroad, which same is a lie as we all know." He sat back and wiped his mouth with the back of his hand. "You from Linn County, Kansas, maybe?"

"That's right," Kirby said. "How did you know?"

"I knew several Jayhawkers," Elliot said evasively, and was silent.

Elliot probably knew more about the underground railroad than he was saying. That was a good test of the man, Kirby thought. The braggers were men like Sam Riley, usually making the most of a small accomplishment.

"Have you counted noses yet?" Kirby asked.

"You aim to pin me down, don't you, son?" Elliot laughed shortly. "Well, I've been doing a little counting in the back of my head while we've been jawing and chawing out o' the front. You tell Martin it looks to me like fifty-fifty if the talk is any sign, but as to how many will fight, hell, I ain't no son of a seventh son. I don't figure me or you or even Martin Kane will know till the shooting starts."

Kirby nodded, for that was exactly what he had thought all the time.

"Where you going from here?" Elliot asked.

"Gold Hill."

"And from there?"

"Golden City and the little burgs around there, and after that the Gregory Gulch diggings."

Elliot clucked sympathetically. "He give you a time limit?"

"No."

"Good. Now I ain't being disrespectful of Martin. He's the kind of man we need in the place he's in. I reckon years from now when some smart professor writes a history book and tells all about this, he won't have no mention of Martin Kane, but if Jefferson Territory comes in as a free state, it'll be due to what Martin does in the next five, six months."

Elliot sopped a piece of biscuit in the grease in his

plate, ate it, and scowled as if suddenly realizing he had talked too much. Kirby restrained a smile, for he guessed the same fear was in Elliot's mind that had been in his own a few minutes ago, that what was being said here might get back to Kane.

"I just aimed to say that he's a pretty hard man at times," Elliot said. "Now if you was told to ride on to Gold Hill in the morning, you'd be in a tolerable hard fix with this storm hitting like it is. Seeing as you don't know the country, you might do good to stay another day with me."

"We'll see how it is in the morning," Kirby said.

The clouds were still hanging low when daylight came reluctantly to a chilled, white world. The temperature was close to zero, but there was not more than three inches of dry, powdery snow on the ground. Kirby decided to try going on, and told Elliot he'd be back to stay with him if the snow was too deep for safe traveling.

Kirby walked to the stable, saddled his buckskin, and rode up the creek. He stopped at Elliot's cabin to clarify the directions the stableman had given him, then rode on into the canyon, the steep, granite walls closing in on him.

EIGHTEEN

KIRBY found that the snow became deeper the higher he climbed, but only on the last mile was there enough to bother his horse. He dismounted and, leading his buckskin, broke trail, and so reached Gold

Hill late in the afternoon. It took another half hour to find the cabin of Tony Harms, the man he had come to see.

Harms was a good-natured, friendly man, short and wide-faced and a little on the pudgy side. He shook hands with Kirby, and said, "I'll have supper ready in a jiffy. Put your animal up in the shed back of the cabin and come in."

Later in the evening when Kirby asked him the questions Martin Kane wanted answered, he found that Harms was not as good-natured as he had first thought. He was openly critical of Kane for sending Kirby out in weather like this to ask questions that couldn't be answered with any degree of certainty. He ended up by guessing at the answers, saying that 90 percent of the Gold Hill miners were for the Union, and if it came to a fight, he would personally raise a company.

Kirby could not bring himself to ask the question that had been nagging him for weeks until after breakfast the following morning. Then, just before he left the cabin to saddle his buckskin, he asked, "Do you know Duke Rome?"

Harms eyed him a moment from under bushy brows, then he said carefully, "Yeah, I know him."

"You know his wife Laurie?"

Harms chewed on his lower lip a moment, his eyes boring into Kirby for several seconds before he said in the same guarded tone, "Yeah, I know her."

"How do they get along?"

Then Harms exploded. He hammered the tabletop with the calloused palm of his hand, making the dishes rattle. "What in hell are you asking me for? Find out for yourself. Leave your horse in the shed and climb to the top of the ridge. You'll find the snow purty deep going up, but when you get there, you probably won't find much because it catches every damned breeze that blows. That's where Rome built their cabin and that's where you'll find his wife."

"How do they get along?" Kirby asked again.

"Ask her, I tell you. Ask him if you can find him, which you probably won't. He'll be off playing cards somewhere."

"All right," Kirby said. "I'll go see her, but maybe she won't tell me the truth."

Harms jammed his hands into his pockets, and walked to the window. He stared at the spruce trees with their drooping boughs burdened by snow, then turned slowly to face Kirby. "You Laurie's friend?"

Kirby nodded. "I knew her in Kansas. She was in the same wagon train I was. I've worried about her ever since I heard her pa was killed and she married Rome."

Harms wiped his face with his right hand, then threw it out in a violent gesture. "Grant, I never felt so helpless about anything in my life. It's a situation where you're damned if you do and damned if you don't. I feel sorry for her, and I wish I could do something for her. So do most of the other men in camp, the decent ones anyhow. But it's none of our business. Just don't seem to be the kind of thing we ought to interfere with."

"Does he beat her? Or abuse her in any way?"

"No," Harms said. "We'd hang him if he did. She never complains, she works like a dog, and she looks like she'd blow off the top of the mountain if she stepped outside her cabin, but she don't never seem to be sick."

"Most miners' wives have a tough life. I don't see why—"

"Sure, sure," Harms interrupted, "and we wouldn't feel the way we do if Rome was worth a damn, but he ain't. He's taken up with three cronies who seem to have money. They buy the grub. Mrs. Rome cooks for 'em and does their washing and ironing in exchange for three meals a day. It's the only way she and Rome would get a meal."

"I'm not surprised about Duke," Kirby said.

"If you're an old friend, you ought to go see her," Harms said. "She don't get to visit with other women 'cause there ain't any others up here on top." He hesitated, then he added, "I reckon we feel sorry for her 'cause she's such a frail, pathetic-looking woman. I've seen whipped dogs like that. They want to be loved, and all the time they're afraid you're going to haul off and give 'em another kick."

"She's always been that way," Kirby said. "Even her pa wasn't any good. Well, I'll go see her."

Kirby floundered to the top of the ridge through knee-deep snow, not seeing any tracks until he reached the crest, then discovered that several men had left the cabin which was perched precariously on the very tip of the ridge directly ahead of Kirby. Only an inept man would build in such a place, but Duke Rome was that kind of man.

Kirby paused, glancing up at the sky which was a sharp, almost dazzling blue without a trace of a cloud anywhere. For this moment at least there was no wind.

The thin air was very cold, probably below zero, possessing a strange, brittle quality that gave Kirby a weird feeling. Perhaps it was the awesome silence. For some crazy reason he had a notion that the earth was frozen, and a sudden sound or movement would cause it to open up in a great crack and swallow him and the cabin and Laurie if she were in it.

He had to admit that there was a breathtaking beauty to this scene. The mountains were all around him, the green of the pines and the spruce mixed with the white of the snow. Here and there was a patch of quakies that resembled gray skeletons, now that their leaves were gone. To the west were the great peaks of the Continental Divide, lifting their barren crests above the gentle, timber-covered slopes below them.

He walked toward the cabin, thinking that the beauty Laurie saw every day was not enough. The loneliness would drive anyone crazy.

He knocked on the door. Laurie opened it and stood staring at him, her eyes wide, her mouth open as if the shock of seeing him had paralyzed her. She cried, "Kirby," and threw herself at him. She hugged and kissed him, then she pulled him inside and shut the door and kissed him again. She drew back and looked at him, and began to cry.

"Now hold on," Kirby said. "I didn't come here to make you cry. I happened to be in Gold Hill on business. Suzy told me you and Duke were living here. Well, I just wanted to see you before I went back to Boulder."

"I'm glad you came, Kirby," she whispered. "I'm awful glad. Here, let me have your hat and coat. Sit down at the table. I've got some coffee left from breakfast. I'll heat it up."

He handed her his hat and coat. She laid them on the bunk in the corner that was covered by pine boughs, then turned to the stove and moved the coffeepot from the back to the front. Kirby sat down, glancing around at the barren interior of the cabin: the crude tables and benches, the shelves with their tin plates and cups and pots and pans, and the little cookstove which seemed too small for five people.

Laurie set two cups on the table, then dropped onto a bench across from him and stared at him. She said in a low tone, "I'm sorry I cried, Kirby. It's just that for a moment you were like a glimpse from home. I wish we'd stayed in Kansas. Pa would be alive if we had. It's funny how a person don't know when he's well off."

"This is no way for you to live, Laurie," Kirby said. "I stayed last night with Tony Harms. He told me you were cooking for several men besides Duke."

"Just three others," she said. "It's no trouble. Duke is good about getting in the wood for me. The cabin's small, so I don't have much housework."

"You're as skinny as a fence rail, Laurie," he said. "Don't you get enough to eat, or do you work so hard you wear the fat all off?"

"Oh, Kirby!" she cried. "You know I've never been fat. I feel fine."

He had to admit that she did not look much different from the way she had always looked. She was right. She never had been fat. Still, this was a poor life for her, taking from her the pride she had once felt in her personal appearance and making a drudge out of her. She had not paid any attention to her hair except to pin it up to get it out of the way. Her cheeks and lips were pale; her dress had been washed in strong soap so often that it had lost its original color and was an ugly gray.

"Are you happy with Duke, Laurie?" Kirby asked. "If you're not, I'll take you back to Denver."

She rose and, picking up the coffeepot from the stove, filled both cups. She shoved one across the table toward Kirby, took the pot back to the stove and returned to the bench where she had been sitting.

"We're getting along fine," she said dully. "Duke doesn't have a job right now. He had one in a mill when we first came, but it was up on top and they didn't have enough water, so they're going to move it down to Left Hand Creek in the spring and he'll go back to work. He's talking about working an arrastra wheel between now and then."

Kirby picked up his cup and drank the coffee, his gaze on the girl's face. No, she wasn't happy, he thought. Her discontent was easy to read in her eyes, in the somber downturn of the corners of her mouth.

"You still haven't answered my question," he said. "Do you want to leave Duke? Do you want to go back to Denver with me?"

She couldn't look at him. On the table in front of her, her hands fisted and opened and fisted again. Finally she said, "No, I don't want to go back to Denver with you. I guess I'm not happy, but then I never have been. I married Duke, and I'll stay with him as long as he stays with me."

She had some pride left, he thought, enough to make her remember that he had warned her against marrying

Duke. He rose. "All right, Laurie, if that's what you want. I've got to get started back down the mountain. If you ever need help, go to Tony Harms."

"I will, Kirby," she said listlessly.

She did not move from the table as he put on his coat and hat and buckled his gun belt around his coat. He stood at the door for a moment looking at her and thinking how different she was from Suzy.

"Good-bye, Laurie," he said.

"Good-bye, Kirby."

She did not look at him. He opened the door and went out, closing it behind him. She was, as Tony Harms had said, a frail, pathetic-looking girl. She tugged at a man's heartstrings, but as he turned away, the thought struck him that she was the kind who was born to be unhappy, that she never had been and never would be any other way.

"Kirby."

He looked up to see Duke Rome standing twenty feet in front of him, the sheer shock of seeing him here apparently paralyzing the man.

"How are you, Duke?" Kirby said. "I've been visiting with Laurie."

Rome's face, red from the cold, now turned almost purple with fury. "You came sucking around her again, didn't you? You knew we was married, but that didn't stop you. I ought to kill you."

"Go ahead," Kirby said. "You're wearing a gun. Pull it. All I want is an excuse to make a widow out of Laurie. I'll take her to Denver and she can find a job. Looks to me like any kind of life would be better than what you're giving her." He paused, watching Rome back away, then he added, "I asked her if she wanted to go to Denver with me, but she said she was going to stay with you. I'm damned if I know why."

Rome didn't act as if he'd heard. He yelled, "Don't you ever come back here again. Don't you ever try to see her. I ain't a man to share my wife with you. Now you get out of here."

Kirby moved toward him. He said, "You were going to kill me, Duke. You'll never have a better chance."

Rome continued to retreat, moving faster now, and being careful to keep his right hand away from his gun. "By God, I will kill you someday," he screamed.

He whirled and plunged into the timber and disappeared. For a time Kirby stood staring thoughtfully after him. He had had the wild hope that by challenging Rome, he might make him act the part of a man, say he'd take Laurie away and support her the way a wife should be supported, but as Kirby started down the trail toward Tony Harms's cabin, he knew that all he had done was to make Rome hate him more than ever. Kirby did not doubt that Rome had meant what he'd said about killing him. Now he had another enemy, a very dangerous one because he was a coward.

NINETEEN

KIRBY stopped overnight with Henry Elliot after leaving Gold Hill. The following morning he left for Golden City, and from there he went on to Gregory Gulch. He returned to Denver on a warm afternoon three days before Christmas.

He left his buckskin at the Elephant Corral, took a room again in the Broadwell House where he shaved, had a bath, and changed clothes. He ate supper, and then walked through the darkness to the Jones cabin. When he knocked, Suzy opened the door and peered at him for a moment. Recognizing him in the thin light from the lamp which was on the table behind her, she screamed, "Kirby," and threw herself at him.

Suzy kissed him, pulled him inside and shut the door, and pounced on him again. She drew her lips from his and tipped her head back to look at him. She said, "Kirby, did I ever tell you that you are a beautiful man?"

"Oh, come on, woman." He scratched his long nose, he pulled his lower lip out so it bulged over the upper one, then rubbed his jutting jaw. "You could pay me a compliment that's true. I like to be flattered, but I know I'm not beautiful."

"It's a matter of opinion," she said gaily. "I'm prejudiced, but I think you're beautiful."

"Now I could say you were beautiful, and I'd be telling the truth," he said.

"Oh, you can do better than that."

"All right, you're a good cook. You keep a neat house. You're a shapely wench. Your clothes show you have excellent tastes. Your perfect figure is evident to my discerning eye."

"That's enough," she said, suddenly embarrassed. "Along that line, I mean, but I say you can still do better."

He pulled at an ear, grinning. "How's this? You're like a loaded revolver, cocked, with a hair trigger."

"That's it." She giggled. "I knew you could think of something good. Take off your coat and hat. You're going to stay awhile, aren't you?"

"I'll stay as long as you'll let me."

"That would be forever, and you know it." She took his hat and coat and laid them on her brother's bed as she asked, "Can I get you a cup of coffee? Or a piece of cake? I have a mince pie I just took out of the oven."

"Maybe later," he said. "Right now I want to know what's happened since I left."

"Oh, the usual fighting and killing," she said, her tone bitter. "Sometimes I wonder if the people who came to Denver were all brutes back home, or if they got that way after they moved out here."

He thought about it a moment, then he said, "I've seen some bad things since I left Denver. We live a rough life out here from necessity. There aren't many decent women in the territory. I have a notion that women make brutal men a little less brutal."

"And the ones who aren't decent make them more brutal." She shrugged. "But maybe I'm being unfair. Bill says I should quit baking for the houses that I've been doing business with. He thinks I see too much of the bad side of life, and I'm so busy I don't get a chance to see the good."

"Maybe he's right," Kirby said. "You don't have to have the money, do you?"

She shook her head. "We could get along till summer. Or I could put out a sign and do my baking for people who come in off the streets, but Martin Kane won't let me. He says that he wants a spy who can come and go without being suspected, and that sooner or later I'll learn something important. I guess he's right."

"He's not right enough to make you unhappy," Kirby said. "Or to make you do things and go places that you shouldn't."

"Oh, I'll be all right." She pulled a chair toward the stove and motioned for him to sit down. When he did, she dropped down on his lap. "We had a killing that was a bad one. You probably heard about it. Charley Harrison shot a rancher named James Hill in the Criterion. There was a good deal of conflicting evidence given at the trial, Bill says. It seemed that most of the important people of Denver were involved. They finally had a ten-to-two jury vote for acquittal and dismissed the case. After it was over the story was whispered around that Ada LaMont had scattered five thousand dollars in the right places so the jury wouldn't agree. I never had enough gall to ask her if it's true, but I can believe it."

He nodded. It was the kind of justice that could be expected if Charley Harrison's life was at stake.

"Now tell me about your trip," Suzy said. "Did you see the men Kane wanted you to see?"

"All of them," Kirby said. "I was caught in some bad storms a time or two, but most of the time I made out all right. I suppose I'd better tell Kane what I found out."

"He's not in town," she said. "Bill and Randy Curl are with him. I don't know where they are, but Bill told me to tell you if you got in before they came back you were to stay in town and wait to report to Kane."

"I suppose they're trying another man like Archibald Bland," Kirby said harshly, "and after they try him, they'll kill him."

"No, it isn't that," she said. "Bill wouldn't say what they were going to do. He keeps telling me that the less I know, the better off I am. I guess he's right, but I picked up the idea that this trip has something to do with guns. If the secesh crowd is able to buy almost all the guns and powder and percussion caps in the territory, they could make it hard on us."

She had been leaning her head against his chest, and his arms were around her. Now he pushed her away and, placing a hand on her chin, turned her head so he could see her face. He asked, "Are you serious?"

"I'm not sure," she answered. "I just got the notion that Bill was real worried, and I thought something like that could be the reason."

"It'd be enough to worry a man," he said. "I never thought they could do anything like that, but if they can—" His voice trailed off. He still couldn't believe it.

His trip to the camps had proved to him that in numbers the Free Soilers and the proslavery men were about equally divided, but if there were any advantage, it lay with the secesh people because it seemed to Kirby that they were better organized. He could not tell Martin Kane, but he had a conviction they were also better led. That, he thought, could be the work of Dave Thorn.

"Kirby?"

"Yes?"

She had leaned her head against his chest again. Now she asked in a low tone, "Did you see Laurie?"

"I saw her a little while one morning," he said. "I offered to bring her to Denver, but she said she was going to stay with Duke as long as he stayed with her. She's awfully thin, but she seems to feel all right. She's living in a cabin with Duke and cooking for three other men. I wish we could do something for her, but I don't know what it would be."

"She could come here and live with Bill and me," Suzy said. "By now she's probably going to have a baby, and she doesn't have any money."

"I'm sure she doesn't," Kirby said. "I'm also sure she wouldn't come. Not now, anyway."

He turned her head again and kissed her. He had never loved her as much as he did in that moment. Feeling as she did about Laurie, and still offering to let her live here, showed a wonderful generosity.

"I love you, Suzy," he said. "I love you very much. Let's get married now."

"Kane won't let us," she said angrily. "I asked him just before he left."

He didn't press it, but he decided he would talk to Kane himself.

TWENTY

KIRBY searched Denver for an engagement ring, but he did not find one until the afternoon of the day before Christmas. By sheer good luck he ran into a peddler who had just returned from the camps in South Park. The diamond was small, but it glittered with flashing brilliance when the sunlight caught it, and to Kirby it was perfect.

"It's never been worn," the peddler said. "I came out

here from St. Louis last summer, bringing along some geegaws that cost me a sight of money. I got rid of all of 'em but this one. I guess there just ain't enough men who struck it rich."

"I didn't strike it rich," Kirby said, "but I've got a girl who'd like to get married."

He took the ring to a jeweler on Larimer Street who examined it and said the diamond was genuine and the ring was gold. He bought it, and gave it to Suzy after supper on Christmas Eve. She cried when he slipped it on her finger, and said it was the best Christmas present she'd ever had. She lay still in his arms a long time, then she stirred and sat up.

"Kirby, are you sure you want to marry me?" Suzy asked.

"Of course I'm sure. You think I'd buy a ring like that if I wasn't?"

"I don't know what to think sometimes," she said miserably. "I've done everything wrong with you. I'm ashamed of myself, but I couldn't seem to help it."

"What do you mean, you've done everything wrong?" he demanded.

"I've been too forward," she said. "At first you didn't even notice me—"

She stopped as if unable to put her thought into words. He pulled her to him and kissed her, then he said, "Maybe I like a forward woman."

She lay in his arms, her eyes closed. He went on. "I noticed you, all right, but I didn't think it was time for me to fall in love with any woman. Martin Kane's right about one thing. We're in a war and we're in the army, and we may get killed. I didn't want to get married and leave a widow, or even to fall in love and bring sadness to a girl who loved me."

"If you're killed, it will bring sadness to me whether we're married or not." She was silent a moment, then she said vehemently, "I hate Martin Kane. I want to be married now. I would rather have a little happiness and be a widow than to not be a widow. There's no merit in trying to avoid sadness. It wouldn't make me happy, Kirby."

He hadn't thought of it that way before. He said, "I'll talk to Kane when I make my report."

"And if you defy him," she whispered, "he will decide you are to be killed. We're caught, Kirby. Don't you see? He thinks he's God."

He felt an unexpected chill ravel down his backbone. Suzy was right. Martin Kane was neither God nor an agent of a legal government empowered to decide who should live or die. In a sudden flash of insight, he sensed that a day of judgment lay ahead for him, a day when he must decide what his values were. He would live or die by that decision.

He did not tell Suzy this. He said again, "I'll talk to Kane when I make my report."

Christmas was a pleasant day; the sky was brilliant blue, the air pleasantly warm. Kirby was amazed by the climate of this country. It could produce a violent snowstorm early in the fall, and a month later bring a Christmas day as balmy as if it were Indian summer.

When Kirby arrived at the Jones's cabin, he saw that Suzy had the windows and doors open. The smell that came to him the moment he stepped inside started his mouth watering. She had set the table with her best china; her cut glass and silver glittered so brightly that he hid his eyes behind his hands.

"It's blinding," he said. "I'll never see again."

"Oh, you fool," she said, laughing. "Come in and look. This is only a sample of the luxury we'll have after we're married."

She'd bought a turkey from a man who had brought a load to Denver from the southern part of the territory. In addition, she had gravy and stuffing and potatoes, and a custard pie for dessert.

When he had eaten so much he was in misery, he said, "You are a rare jewel. I won't let you escape me. If any man comes around making eyes at you, I'll kill him dead."

She snapped her fingers. "Just like that. I should tell you, kind sir. I don't want to be let go."

"Well then—" He paused to groan and pat his stomach, and went on, "I guess we are in complete agreement."

"Go lie down on Bill's bed and take a nap," she said. "I'll join you as soon as I do the dishes."

That night they went to Apollo Hall for the pantomime, "The Golden Ox." The place was jammed, and Kirby noted that the crowd had a larger proportion of women than usual.

The following week Kirby relaxed and enjoyed life. He took Suzy to plays and to a concert by the Excelsior Band in the Broadwell House. Suzy said nothing about her brother, but Kirby knew that she was concerned; she had expected him home before this.

Bill came in late New Year's Eve just after midnight, dirty, tired, bearded, and hungry. Suzy built up the fire and cooked a meal for him. He dropped into a chair beside the stove and looked at Kirby, weariness cutting deep lines into his face.

"I'm so tired I don't have good sense," he said, "but I remember Martin gave me a message for you. If I saw you, I was to tell you he wanted a report tomorrow."

"All right," Kirby said, "he'll get it."

"We had one hell of a rough trip," Bill said. "We'd had a report that Dave Thorn was buying up all the percussion caps in the country, and had 'em stored in a cabin up the South Platte, but we sure didn't find 'em. You're not to repeat this to anybody, but I thought you ought to know in case you'd heard about it and had some information."

Kirby shook his head. "It's news to me."

"Bill." Suzy turned from the stove to face him. "I know you're in no mood to talk, but I'm going to tell you anyway." She showed him her ring. "Isn't it beautiful?"

"It sure is." Bill kissed his sister and shook hands with Kirby. "I ain't surprised much. I reckon the way you two felt about each other wasn't no secret."

"No, we didn't intend for it to be a secret," Suzy said. "That's what I'm going to talk to you about. We want to get married now, and we agree that it's none of Martin Kane's business."

"Oh, my God," Bill groaned. "Sis, we've gone over this a dozen times. I thought we was finished with it."

"It won't be finished until we're married," she said sharply. "You haven't talked to Kirby about it?"

"No I haven't." Bill turned to Kirby. "How about it? This all Suzy's idea in trying to herd you to the altar in such a big hurry?"

"Bill!" Suzy cried. "You make me so damned mad."

"No, it's not all her idea," Kirby said. "What's more, I aim to let Kane know how we feel when I make my report."

"All right," Bill said wearily. "If you're bound to tell him, I can't stop you, so go ahead and have your say."

That was all he said, but it was enough to tell Kirby that the words were intended to be a warning.

TWENTY-ONE

KIRBY slept late on New Year's Day, so that it was nearly noon by the time he'd had breakfast and had shaved. He hesitated about going to Kane's at that hour, but decided he couldn't put it off. He wanted to have something to tell Suzy, although he wasn't sure what it would be.

Kane was drinking coffee when Kirby knocked on his door. He hadn't shaved, his eyes were red-rimmed, and he looked as tired as Bill Jones had the night before.

"Come in, Grant," Kane said as he shook hands. "When did you get back?"

"A little while before Christmas," Kirby answered.

"We left about that time." Kane shut the door and motioned to a chair. "Sit down and I'll pour you a cup of coffee." He tapped a stack of newspapers that was on the table. "We were gone almost two weeks, so I'm behind in my reading. I'm not sure how much influence the newspapers carry, but at least they tell us how certain men feel. Byers expresses himself in the *News*. So does Coleman in the *Mountaineer*."

He set a tin cup on the table, filled it with coffee, and put it back on the stove. Kirby, studying him, felt again that this man could assume any personality he thought fitted the occasion. First he had been the faceless miner, then the strong man controlling the words and decisions and perhaps even the thoughts of the others in the room. Now, at this third meeting, he was a nervous man, worried and tense, a fine machine so tightly wound that even his hands trembled as he poured the coffee.

He sat down across the table from Kirby, and tapped the pile of newspapers again. "Perhaps you know that South Carolina has seceded. Other Southern states are sure to follow, and that makes war inevitable. The South is not a rich section, and a war takes money. I feel sure it will do its best to conquer Colorado for its gold, and from here they can cut California off from the rest of the Union and have its mines as well."

Kane leaned forward, his gaze fixed on Kirby's face. "Most of our editors are Northern in sympathy, but they are inclined to argue that nothing very important or terrible will happen. On the other hand, James Coleman says plainly and boldly that if the South follows South Carolina, the West will go along. Utah has reason to hate the federal government. California and Oregon have powerful Southern leaders who will try to take them out of the Union and form a Pacific Republic."

Kane pounded on the table and raised his voice. "By God, this may be exactly what will happen if we don't stop it. Since the federal government has not recognized Jefferson Territory—in fact, has completely ignored the entire Pikes Peak country—Coleman may be right in saying it will go with the South."

Kane sat back and wiped a hand across his bearded face. "I'll admit I'm worried. Did Bill tell you what we were doing on this trip?" Kirby nodded, and Kane went on, "Our information may have been wrong. Or the percussion caps may have been so well hidden we couldn't find them. The trouble is we may wake up some morning to find the secesh crowd well armed and in control of the city, while the rest of us have only a smattering of guns and practically no caps."

Kane picked up his tin cup and drank his coffee, his eyes glittering under his heavy brows. Kirby thought again that Martin Kane might be a fanatic in his way just as John Brown and Archibald Bland had been, and James Montgomery was now. The strange part of the situation was that Kane did not view himself in that light. He considered the men he called "fanatics" dangerous men, but he looked upon himself as a cool-headed leader who could bring the Pikes Peak mining country into the Northern camp and keep it in the Union.

To Kirby there was little if anything that was new in what Kane had said, and it irritated him that he must sit here and listen to a tirade that did nothing but ease the tension that was in Martin Kane. Kirby saw no reason to wait until Kane got around to asking him for his report, so he said, "Bill told me you wanted my report today."

Kane gave a start as if suddenly and rudely jolted back to reality. "Yes," he said. "Yes, of course."

Kirby started with the night he had spent in Boulder with Henry Elliot, and finished with his last night in Black Hawk in the Gregory diggings. He finished with, "Golden City was the only place where I felt the Southerners were in the majority. In most of the camps, I'd say it was fifty-fifty, and in a few like Gold Hill the Northerners were in the majority. However, it's like Henry Elliot said. This is only a guess on the part of the men I talked to. I suppose they made their judgment on the basis of talk they overheard in the saloons. Elliot answered your question about how many would fight for the North by saying no one could know until the shooting started."

"Of course," Kane said absently. "Of course."

Anger stirred in Kirby as he rose. He had the feeling that Martin Kane had only half listened to what he had said. Now, as he picked up his hat from where he had laid it on the table, he said, "Suzy and I plan to get married now."

"No." Kane's face turned white as he jumped to his feet. "I forbid it. I told Suzy that. You are soldiers in an army, and are sworn to do your duty as you are commanded. I have work for both of you to do."

"We're not trying to get out of any work," Kirby said, "but we can do it married as well as single."

"No, that's where you're wrong," Kane shot back. "Once you're married, you'll be concerned about yourself and each other. I can't have that. You must be concerned first and foremost about the cause we're fighting for."

"We will be concerned." Kirby paused, struggling to keep control of his temper. "I can't see that even a general has a right to say whether his privates can get married or not."

Kane's lips thinned and tightened against his teeth. He was obviously not used to defiance, and Kirby wasn't sure he could control himself. He remained silent for several seconds, then he said, "Grant, this is an order. You will leave for the South Park camps at dawn tomorrow morning."

Shocked, Kirby stood motionless, staring at Kane as he lifted the stack of newspapers and picked up a sheet of paper that had been under it. On the paper was written the names of men and the camps in which they lived.

"You will do the same as you did on this other trip," Kane said. "Notice that some of these camps are over the range from South Park. At this time of year the weather will be against you, so take your time. Do not report back until you have covered the ground. The only exception to that order is that if you come onto any exact information concerning the percussion caps that Dave Thorn is supposed to be storing, return to Denver at once."

Kirby glanced at the paper, folded it, and slipped it into his pocket. He was over his shock and thinking coherently now. He suspected that Kane had just now thought of assigning him to this trip, and was using it to keep him from marrying Suzy. There must be men available who knew the country better than he did—if indeed any more checking was necessary. If Kane was in love with Suzy, this order could be another effort to rid himself of a rival. He wondered again if Kane had been responsible for the attempt John Deal had made on his life in Boulder. But these were wild suspicions, and it would be stupid to face Kane with them unless he had proof.

"All right," Kirby said. "I have one more thing to say. You've got to tell Suzy to quit taking the business of the brothels. She hasn't heard anything of importance, and she's seeing too much of the bad side of life."

"No, I won't do that," Kane said sharply. "We never know what she'll hear. Men like Charley Harrison frequent those places. If they're a little drunk, they'll talk too much. She has a better chance of bringing us important information than Bill has."

"If they find out her connection with you," Kirby said, "they'll kill her."

"Perhaps they will," Kane agreed, "but that is no reason to move her from an important assignment. They'll kill Bill if they find out who he really is, and they'll kill you if they think it's necessary. God knows they'd kill me today if they knew who I am. That's one important advantage we have. We know who Dave Thorn is, but they don't know who I am."

"Suzy's a woman," Kirby said angrily. "You can't risk her life the same as you would mine or Bill's or yours."

"Yes I can," Kane shot back. "She knew the risks when she took the job. A life is a life, Grant, whether it's male or female. What we're trying to do is too important to haggle over whether that life belongs to a man or a woman."

"God have pity on you if this costs Suzy her life," Kirby said in a low tone, "because I won't."

He clapped his hat on and left the cabin. In spite of Kane's order not to go to the Jones place in daylight when Bill was home, Kirby went there immediately and told Suzy and her brother about the order he had received.

"That's a hell of a job to tackle this time of year," Bill said. "They get some winter weather in South Park that nobody travels in."

"That's the chance I've got to take," Kirby said, "and I'm willing to take it, but why does he act the way he does about Suzy and me getting married?"

"I can't really tell you," Bill said, "but I can tell you he insists on obedience. He's convinced that it's the only way we can act effectively and do the job we came here to do."

Kirby put his arm around Suzy. He thought about saying that he had tried to get her removed from the dangerous assignment Kane had given her, and decided against it. Bill understood, and still had not done anything, so there was nothing Kirby could do. He also decided against mentioning his suspicion that Kane was in love with her. Before he returned from South Park, Kane might declare himself, then they would know.

"Suzy calls Kane a madman," Kirby said. "I had the same feeling today. He had the wild look in his eyes that I've seen in James Montgomery's. I thought it was the expression of a fanatic, but maybe it's more the look of a hunted man."

Bill shook his head. "He's not a fanatic, not in the sense John Brown was. I wouldn't follow him if I thought he was. I don't think your friend Montgomery is that bad, either, but they are hunted men, so you might be right. Kane is ruthless, he's arrogant, and he's tough. Above everything else, he's bound to save the Union if he sacrifices every one of us. That's the only reason I'm still with him."

"We'll wait, darling," Suzy said. "I'm sorry I pressed you about getting married. I knew better."

"We'll wait till I get back anyway," Kirby said. "After that we'll see."

He left at dawn the following morning, his blankets tied behind his saddle. He was not at all sure he would ever see Suzy again.

TWENTY-TWO

THE good weather held for the first two or three days after Kirby left Denver. The nights were cold, but not so cold that they presented any danger; the skies were usually clear during the days, with a bright sun that gave little heat to the chilled earth. Although the air held an expected winter bite, Kirby was not uncomfortable except when a wind drove at him from the white-topped peaks to the west. Fortunately he had to face very little wind during those first days.

Snow covered the ground, varying from an inch or so to a foot deep. Kirby kept his face blackened with charcoal, and when the sun seemed unusually bright he wore a black mask. Tony Harms had showed him the trick with the charcoal, and had given him the mask before he left Gold Hill. Carelessness had blinded more than one man when snow was on the ground and a dazzling sun was overhead, Harms had said.

Kirby hoped to reach the camps on the west side of the Park before a storm struck, but when he topped Kenosha Pass and looked out across the vast expanse of South Park, he knew his good luck wasn't going to hold. Ominous black clouds covered the sky, with a sullen steel coloring appearing along the western edge above the peaks.

It was after noon now; there was no wind, no movement that he could see anywhere in the vast stretch of country below him. The absolute silence was even more awesome than it had been the morning he had stood on top of the ridge at Gold Hill before going into Laurie's cabin.

He struck off down the slope, knowing he was at about ten thousand feet and at such an altitude the approaching storm could be a man-killer. The wind had swept the snow off the frozen ground in a number of places, and when his buckskin's hoofs hit such a spot, Kirby noticed how the sound rattled and echoed all around him through the thin air.

Within an hour the strange steel coloring had worked across the sky. For the first time in his life Kirby was afraid of the weather. He didn't know whether anybody lived on this side of the Park or not, but he did know he was a long way from the mining camps.

He considered turning north before it was dark to hunt for some sort of protection in the timber that covered the neighboring hills, then decided against it. He knew that these storms sometimes lasted for days. If this one did, neither he nor the buckskin would make it.

He headed straight across the Park, thinking that his only chance was to find a cabin before it was too dark to see anything. The sky had steadily darkened, filtering the sunlight so it seemed like dusk, although it was still early in the afternoon. Suddenly the thought struck him that this was exactly what Martin Kane hoped would happen. He'd be a good man if he got through the storm alive, and he told himself he'd show Kane that was exactly the kind of man he was.

A hard wind had sprung up, bringing with it the first tiny flakes of snow that stung his cheeks. The wind destroyed the silence. It made a noise that was more terrifying than silence, a steady, shrill scream that filled the air as a roaring flood would do.

The peaks to the west had been lost to sight for quite a while. Now the hills to the north were gone, too. In another minute or so the snow was falling so hard that it formed a white wall around him, and he could not see more than ten feet in any direction. He realized then that he had lost his sense of direction. He might be drifting south, and if he was, he would soon be a dead man because the Park ran for miles, desolate and empty.

Kirby tried to pull his buckskin to the right, thinking that north lay that way. Perhaps it was not too late to find the timber and a shielded ravine where he would have some protection through the night at least. The horse refused to obey. Kirby thought, "We've been going in a circle."

For one terrible, heart-stopping moment he lost all hope; they would go around in a great circle until they both froze to death. The next moment another thought struck him. In a situation like this an animal figured things out before a human did. The horse knew what to do and where to go better than he did. After that he made no attempt to guide the buckskin.

The snow was coming down harder than ever, so hard that he could not suck air into his lungs. He rode with his head tipped down, his right hand raised over his mouth and nose. In this way he was able to breathe.

Time seemed to have stopped. At least he had lost all concept of it. He could do nothing except stay on the horse and hope the snow did not get so deep that it stopped their progress. There had been very little snow on the ground when he had topped Kenosha Pass, but it was piling up fast now.

He felt a deadening cold work through his clothes. He had pulled his scarf around his face, and now ice was forming on the cloth in front of his mouth and nose and on his eyebrows. Once he stepped out of the saddle and walked beside the horse for a time, letting the buckskin lead him. He wasn't thinking clearly now, but he did remember his decision to give the horse his head.

His legs had felt wooden, but he had the circulation going when he swung back into the saddle. He gripped the horn, bending forward again. When he looked up, he could see nothing ahead of him except the V of the horse's ears.

Once more the thought raveled through his numbed brain that he'd be a good man if he got through this alive. He cursed Martin Kane for sending him out on this mission that had no real meaning. He was jarred by a cold pine bough slapping him across the face. He wondered vaguely where he was, then he realized the buckskin had stopped.

A man shook his arm, saying, "Come on, friend. You ain't froze plumb stiff, are you? See if you can get one leg over your horse. I just ain't tall enough to lift you out o' your saddle."

It seemed to Kirby that it took a long time for his brain to telegraph the message to his leg, but eventually his foot started to move. In the end he almost tumbled out of the saddle, and would have fallen into the snow if the man hadn't caught and steadied him.

"That's the stuff," the man said. "You can make those legs move. Just seems like you can't. Make 'em take you inside. We'll get you thawed out."

Kirby had to take only three steps to reach the door, but time was so distorted that it seemed several minutes before he was inside a cabin with the door shut behind him. A lighted candle was on the table in the middle of the room, and on the other side of the table a fire crackled in a cookstove.

"Now I've got to go out and take care of your horse," the man said. "While I'm gone, you walk back and forth along the wall, but don't go to the stove and think you're going to get warmed up in a minute. What you need is time. You've got plenty of it 'cause you're going to be here for quite a spell."

Kirby heard the door open and close. He leaned against the log wall and slowly unwound the scarf from around his face. He wiped the water that ran down his cheeks from his eyebrows where the ice had melted, and then began to walk, stamping his feet to restore the circulation. Suddenly he realized how close he had come to dying.

He was still walking when the man returned. "This one is a booger," he said. "If I didn't have a rope strung between the cabin and the shed, I'd never make it from one to the other." He looked at Kirby for a moment, then he said, "Your horse will be all right. Now let's take your hat and coat off. You can get a little closer to the fire now. We'll see about your boots, too."

Kirby's fingers were still too numb to unbuckle his gun belt, so the man helped him with it, then hung the belt, hat and coat from pegs in the wall. He said, "My name's Barney Bean. I've got a ranch here. In the long run I figure a man's gonna make more money out of cattle than he is out of gold, but you sure can't tell that to most fellers who go by here. Now I reckon you're headed for one of the mining camps, but traveling this time of year makes you about as smart as the greenhorn who bought an ax to cut up buffalo chips. Only thing is you don't look like no greenhorn."

"I'm not," Kirby said. "My name's Kirby Grant. I was headed for the camps, all right, but I'm not after gold."

"Then I guess you had a damned good reason for going," Bean said, "which ain't none of my business, but I'm glad to hear you ain't after gold. It just ain't a good enough reason."

Bean motioned for him to lie on the bunk in the corner, then he tugged off Kirby's boots. He said, "Take off your socks. I'll get some snow."

He picked up a pan and went outside while Kirby carefully rolled down his socks and eased them off his feet.

Bean returned in a moment and rubbed both feet with the snow, then dried them and wrapped them in a wool blanket.

"Soon as the storm lets up so I can get out," Bean said, "I'll cut a balsam sapling. We'll shave off some bark and put a poultice on them feet. I dunno how bad they are, but the best you can figure on is losing a few toenails and some o' your hide. Now I'll cook up a bit of supper. I'll bet a cup of hot coffee would go down right good."

"It would for a fact," Kirby said.

"Funny thing about an animal," Bean said as he bustled around the stove. "You'd have died out yonder in that storm if your horse hadn't found my cabin, 'cause I've got the only one for miles around here. I was just thinking what a hell of a night it was to be out in when I heard your horse. He pawed at the front door or something. Anyhow, I heard him, and opened the door and there you was."

He was grinding coffee, but he stopped long enough to waggle a stubby forefinger at Kirby. "The point is no human being could of found this cabin. Fact is, most men would have figured they knowed more'n the horse, which makes you a sight smarter'n most men. Now there ain't no accounting for a horse doing a thing like that, so I figure the Lord done it, which means he's got use for you."

Kirby's feet were beginning to hurt, but he felt better everywhere else. He hoped his feet were the only part of his body that had suffered any real harm, and that he wouldn't lose any of his toes. He lay on the bunk, listening and watching Bean, a short, heavy-set man who looked as if he had enormous strength in his arms and shoulders. Oddly enough, the lower part of his body tapered down to very small feet. He was well into his fifties, Kirby guessed, but there was no trace of gray in his black hair and thick beard.

Bean winked and picked up a butcher knife and began slicing bacon. He said, "I'm gonna fix you a fine banquet of mountain chicken."

A few minutes later Bean brought him a plate of bacon and rice and three biscuits and a tin cup of steaming coffee. "You stay here on the bunk. No use hobbling around on them bunged-up feet of your'n. They'll give you hell before morning anyhow."

Kirby didn't think he was hungry, but he found himself eating with relish. Bean sat at the table and ate, but he spent more time talking and waving his fork at Kirby to emphasize his points than he did eating.

"I was in Buckskin Joe for a while," Bean said. "I had me a partner, and we had a mine that was looking purty good. Well, I helped him sink the shaft, and then we split our blankets. He bought me out and maybe he'll make a million dollars, but by hokey, I had all I wanted o' grubbin' round in the damn tunnel. I like to see the sun."

After he finished eating, Bean cleaned up the dishes, and said he'd make a bed on the floor for himself. He'd have to keep the fire going or they'd both freeze to death before morning. He grinned and said, "You know, son, when you first got here, you looked like the tail end of a hard winter. Now you're beginning to perk up. I think you'll make it."

"So do I," Kirby said.

He didn't sleep that night. His feet hurt like two giant toothaches, but he gritted his teeth against the groans and grunts that he felt like making. All he had to do was to listen to the wind howling around the cabin, and know that, except for the mercy of God and the instinct of a buckskin horse, he'd be out there in that wind.

TWENTY-THREE

KIRBY remained with Barney Bean for two weeks before he was able to go on. He lost four toenails and much of the skin on both feet, but he was very much aware that he was lucky; he considered it a miracle he was still alive.

He returned to Denver late in April, having spent more than three months in the South Park camps and in California Gulch on the Arkansas. The first thing he heard when he arrived in town was that Fort Sumter had been fired on. Even though he had expected some act of war somewhere in the East, he was shocked when he heard. As he cleaned up in his room in the Broadwell House, he told himself that the worst had finally happened. War had come just as Martin Kane had expected.

He wondered what Kane would do, and then asked himself a more important question. What would Dave Thorn do? He had heard nothing more about Thorn and his supposed efforts to buy up all the percussion caps in the territory, but then it was not likely he would have heard anything about that in the back country camps.

He left the Broadwell House in the cool April twilight and strode along Larimer Street toward Cherry Creek, wondering if Dave Thorn had spies around town who would inform him that Kirby was back, especially if Thorn had not learned the identity of the leader of the Free Soilers. He hadn't been followed when he'd been in Denver at Christmas, though. Perhaps Thorn was too busy with his plans to bother with Kirby Grant's comings and goings.

He wiped his feet carefully before knocking on Suzy's door. A wet spring snow had just gone off the ground the day before and had turned the Denver streets to loblollies. He knocked and the door was opened and Suzy stood there looking at him just as she had at Christmas. She screamed, "Kirby!" and jumped at him, and he caught her in his arms and whirled her around, then put her down and kissed her.

When he let her go, she said breathlessly, "Kirby, I didn't know if you were dead or alive." Then she remembered she was mad at him and she stamped her foot, her face turning red. "Damn you, Kirby Grant. I love you, and I can't wait till we're married, but you didn't bother to even write to me. If you think I'm going to just live here and worry myself to death over a man who—who—" She stopped and began to cry.

He stepped inside and pulled her in after him and closed the door. He said, "Honey, there wasn't a day I didn't think of you. I wrote to you as often as I thought you'd get a letter, but the weather has been hell. I haven't heard from you for over a month."

She stopped crying and stared at him, wide-eyed. Then she said contritely, "I'm so sorry, Kirby. I didn't think that you had a side to this. All I could think of was that you were tearing around from one mining camp to another and some rebel might kill you or you might get buried under an avalanche or freeze to death or something."

Bill stood by the stove, grinning. Now he moved toward Kirby, his hand extended. "Welcome back to Denver, brother-in-law. We've all been wondering about you."

Kirby shook hands with him, knowing there was much he wanted to say to Bill, but knowing, too, that he wanted first of all to be alone with Suzy. He said, "I haven't seen Kane, but I can tell you one thing. We will not put off our marriage any longer."

"Hear, hear," Suzy said skeptically. "I want to see the day when my big old soft-headed brother is actually your brother-in-law, Mr. Kirby Grant. I don't think I'll ever see it because Martin Kane will send you off to New Mexico or Texas or California."

"No he won't," Bill said sharply. "When did you get in, Kirby?"

"This afternoon. I came as soon as I could get a room and clean up."

"Why didn't you come before?" Suzy demanded. "You've made me wait hours before you let me know you were still alive."

"You might not have known I was alive if I'd stopped here when I first got to town," Kirby told her. "I had a beard a foot long, my clothes were worn out, and I smelled like I was a dead goat."

Suzy giggled. "Well, maybe it was a good thing you waited. I'd probably have run away if I'd seen you coming."

"I'll let you two love birds coo," Bill said. "I'll see Martin tonight and I'll tell him you're here. Got any news?"

Kirby shook his head. "Nothing exciting. I didn't hear anything about the percussion caps."

"Neither have we, though we've been looking whenever we had time," Bill said. "Thorn's bought up most of 'em, all right, but we ain't found hide nor hair of 'em. We can't wait much longer. If there's a fight, we'll be caught without enough caps to make much of a scrap."

"Send for some," Kirby said. "You've got freight moving across the plains, haven't you?"

Bill nodded. "We haven't got time to wait for a freight outfit, but we can get some here by express in a few days. We expect the other side to make a move any time, now that the show's started." He scratched his neck, his eyes narrowing. "Only we may make a move before they do. We're Colorado Territory now, you know."

"I heard that Congress finally got around to doing something for us," Kirby said. "It was about time."

"It was more'n time," Bill said grimly. "We still don't have a governor, but we probably will next month. We're the forgotten people, I guess." He moved to the door. "I'll see you tomorrow, Kirby."

He stepped out into the darkness, closing the door behind him. Kirby, turning to Suzy, had the weird feeling that he had lived this moment before, that maybe it would always be this way: he'd leave and tell Suzy good-bye and then he'd come back and kiss her and tell her he loved her and he was going to marry her, but before he could, Martin Kane would find something for him to do.

"Tomorrow," he said. "I'll find a preacher tomorrow. I just won't wait again."

She moistened her lips, then she said ruefully, "We'll probably have to wait a few days, honey, but you go ahead and look for the preacher." She hugged him, her head against his chest as she said softly, "I can't go through it again, waiting this way and not knowing where you are and what's happening to you."

"I don't intend for you to," he said.

She stepped back and, reaching up, patted his cheeks. "Sit down and I'll pour you a cup of coffee. I'm still baking and I'm still doing business with Ada LaMont, but she can wait for this cake until I bake another one in the morning. Sit down and tell me about your trip."

He sat down and briefly told her how it had been, leaving out the time he would have frozen to death in South Park if he hadn't stumbled onto Barney Bean's cabin. When he finished, he asked her to tell him the Denver news.

"A couple of things happened," she said. "We used Washington's birthday to celebrate the Union. We had a flag-raising at Judge Bennett's home, patriotic speeches and the like. They even fired a cannon. I guess we didn't accomplish anything except to let the Southerners know there are a lot of people in Denver who love the Union."

She smiled as she stirred her coffee. "I don't know why I said 'we.' Bill is still supposed to be a Southern sympathizer, and he couldn't go, and I'm not supposed to be interested in politics because I'm still baking for the bad women, so I didn't go."

"You're getting out of that," Kirby said angrily. "I don't know why Bill lets you do it."

She shook her head. "It's not a question of letting me. Kane insists on it, but the day we're married I'm finished. I've told him, and he's agreed." She hesitated, glancing at Kirby, then she said. "The other thing could have been a bloody business. You know Park McClure, the postmaster?"

Kirby nodded, and she went on, "He got a Confederate flag from the South—a real nice one made of silk. McClure wanted folks to admire it, but when he showed it to Judge Waggoner, the Judge spit tobacco juice on it. He says, 'that's what I think of your goddamned flag,' and stomped out of the post office. Bill was there and saw what happened. He told me he thought McClure was going to have a heart attack. For a while it looked as if they'd fight a duel over it, but they didn't."

Suzy spread her hands as if disgusted. "I don't know, Kirby. Sometimes I think these men are a bunch of little boys with their feuds and duels and all, and that there are only a few men like Bill and Martin Kane and you who are really interested in saving the Union, as interested as Dave Thorn is in destroying it."

He reached across the table and took her hands. "I had plenty of chance to do some thinking when I was gone on this trip," he said. "There were weeks at a time when the snow was too deep to go anywhere, so I'd sit in a cabin with some man who might not agree with me politically and we'd have nothing to say to each other or nothing to do but play cards till we got tired of it."

She smiled, "Well, my darling thinker, what did you think?"

"I'd think about you and about the children we'd have, and what I'd do to make a living. I'm going to have to find a job pretty soon." He was silent a moment, then he added, "I guess it was mostly the children I thought about. Out here we don't see any slaves, so it doesn't seem as important to free them as it did when I lived in Kansas, but it still seems important to save the Union.

"I mean, if we lose, there'll be two weak countries who quarrel and fight like the countries in Europe, or maybe even three countries if the Pacific Republic develops. Or else we'll be one strong country the way we are today. I want our children to grow up in that kind of country."

She laughed softly as she squeezed his hand. "Darling, you've done some growing up since I saw you. You weren't thinking about children at Christmas."

"No, I guess not," he said.

She was right, he thought. When a man escapes death as narrowly as he had in South Park, he may mature in a few hours as much as he normally would do in years. He would tell her about it someday, but not now. It was enough just to be alive, and to be with her.

He sensed that she, too, had matured, perhaps due to an adverse fate in the form of Martin Kane. In one way he was glad it had worked out the way it had. They had not been ready for marriage last fall, but they were now.

TWENTY-FOUR

THE following morning Kirby had finished breakfast and left the Broadwell House to go to Martin Kane's cabin when he saw the crowd in front of the Wallingford and Murphy store building. He ran across the dusty intersection of Larimer and G streets, sensing the mob fury of the crowd before he reached it. Then he saw that the men were staring upward at something on top of the building. He tipped his head back and stopped, his heart pounding. A Confederate flag was flying above the store.

For a moment Kirby couldn't move. He heard the roar of the crowd as if from a great distance: oaths, angry cries about tearing the damned rag down, yells about burning the building and hanging Charley Harrison and Park McClure and the rest of the rebel leaders. Some of the men had drawn revolvers or bowie knives, and were waving the weapons over their heads, but none was moving toward the store. The rebel crowd had gathered inside the store, and a few had lined out across the front of the nearby Criterion. Those men, too, would be armed.

If the Union sympathizers attempted to storm the building and tear the flag down, dozens of men would die. In this one fearful moment Kirby had a vision of what would happen if a fight developed. Bill had told him they'd have percussion caps here in a few days. They didn't have them now, but through Dave Thorn's conniving, the rebels did, so they'd win and they'd take possession of Denver. It couldn't happen, Kirby told himself. Not yet.

He lowered his head and, using his strong shoulders and elbows, rammed his way through the crowd. Men cursed him and several raised fists to slug him for his rudeness, but he didn't wait. When he reached the front of the crowd, he saw Martin Kane, tight-lipped and red of face. Randy Curl was standing beside Kane, and on beyond was a man he knew only by sight, Sam Logan.

The bolder spirits among the rebel crowd had spilled forward through the door of the store, and now formed a tight knot. They were silent as they waited, but the crowd behind Kirby continued to make a sullen rumble. It died down as Sam Logan raised his hands over his head.

Logan was a young man, but a bushy growth of hair and his splendid mustache added years to his appearance. He was one who would be listened to, and Kirby, glancing at Kane who was silently staring at Logan, wondered if the bushy-haired man was a member of the Brotherhood.

"I say let's take the store and tear that goddamned rag to shreds," Logan shouted. "Who's with me?"

A dozen men crowded forward, all yelling they were, but the Southern sympathizers in front of the store stood their ground. One man bellowed above the uproar, "You try it. Just try it, and by God, we'll blow your heads off before you get within ten feet of where we're standing."

Kirby grabbed Logan's arm. "Hold on. This isn't the way."

"Stay out of it, Grant," Kane said hoarsely. "We've got

165

to get that symbol of treason down. We can't let it fly over Denver."

Kirby whirled to stare at Kane, unable to believe he'd heard right. Kane knew the situation, yet he was willing to let this come to the point of bloodshed now. He saw the same strange glitter in Kane's eyes he had seen before, and still he wasn't sure whether it indicated that the man was a fanatic or whether it came from the natural fear of one who is hunted by ruthless enemies.

Two other men bulled through the crowd to stand beside Logan. Kirby knew them by sight, too. They were lawyers, Henry Teller and Bela Hughes. Now they started to talk, and the crowd listened.

To bring on a pitched battle out here in the street was a mistake, they argued. Kirby, who had backed up so he could watch both speakers as well as the crowd, saw that the lawyers' calm logic was having its effect. A number of men were moving to the edge of the crowd as if they wanted no part of the fight that seemed inevitable. They were Southerners, Kirby guessed, but men who had no more liking for slavery than he did, and so were caught in a trap of divided loyalties.

In the end all the oratory in the world was not enough to settle emotions that had soared past the stage of reason. A man called, "Let's have someone talk to Wallingford and Murphy. They'll pull the rebel rag down if they know they're gonna get burned out if they don't."

"I'll talk to them." Logan motioned to Kirby and another man Kirby didn't know. "We're a committee. We're not going to wait much longer."

They strode toward the rebel crowd, Logan calling, "We'll give you an hour to haul that flag down. If it isn't down then, we'll take it down. This store building will go, too."

"Don't touch that flag," one of the Southerners snapped back. "It stays where it is."

"Oh, hell," Logan said in disgust. "You can't talk sense into crazy men."

The three men turned and strode back to the Union crowd. Again pistols and knives were waved in the air, and the smell of death was in Kirby's nostrils again. All it would take was for some madman to fire a shot, and the fight would be on. Desperately Kirby turned to Martin Kane, but the man had not moved or said a word. Kirby didn't know why and he had no time to ask. What was to be done had to be done now.

Kirby grabbed Logan's arm and jerked his head at him. He said, "Come here."

Logan hesitated, glancing at Henry Teller. He said, "I don't know why I—"

"Come here," Kirby said fiercely. "Damn it, we don't want a battle, and that's what we're going to get if we don't haul that flag down, so let's get it down."

A grin broke across Logan's face. "Now you're talking," he said. "Come on, Henry."

Teller followed Kirby and Logan around the corner of the building. Kirby pointed to a lean-to shed. "Two of us can boost the third man up on the shed. He can get to the roof of the main building from there, and then it'd be a cinch to pull the flag down."

"I'll do it," Logan said quickly.

Kirby hesitated, wanting to get his hand on the flag so badly it was almost a compulsion in him, but to quarrel with Logan at this time would be stupid. "All right," he said, and looked at Teller, who nodded agreement.

Together Kirby and Teller hoisted Logan high enough for him to scramble to the roof of the shed. They backed off to watch him climb to the top of the store building and make his way to the front, where he yanked the stars and bars from its short staff and ripped it again and again. The crowd in the street cheered as revolvers and knives were shoved back into leather casings.

Kirby ran to the front of the building, expecting Charley Harrison and his pack of toughs to charge out of the Criterion, but they didn't. Slowly the Southerners broke up, some dropping back into the store while the men in front of the Criterion disappeared inside.

Kirby glanced at Teller. He said, "It could have been worse."

The lawyer grinned wryly. "It could indeed," he said, "and it would have if our bunch hadn't got so big that it outnumbered the secesh crowd about two or three to one. They'd have been wiped out if they'd fired a shot, and they knew it."

The crowd in the street began breaking up, Kane and Randy Curl striding along Larimer toward Kane's cabin. Kirby followed, knowing that what he intended to say might be suicide, but he was bound to say it, right or wrong. Kane had had his chance to take command this morning and he had failed, either through cowardice or shortsightedness.

Kirby caught up with them when they reached the

bridge spanning Cherry Creek. Kane glanced around, saw him, and said coldly, "We're glad you're back safely, Grant. If I judge this situation correctly, the fun is about to commence."

"I'll make my report first," Kirby said, "and then I have some things to say. You won't like them, but I'm going to say them anyway."

Kane glanced at Randy Curl as if to say he had expected this. Curl said, "It would be better if you did not say any of them, Grant."

"I'll say them because they've got to be said." Kirby jammed his hands into his pockets. "If Kane wants to call a meeting of the Brotherhood, I'll say it at the assemblage. Otherwise I'll say it now."

Kane's eyes narrowed; his lips were thin and tight against his teeth. He was playing another role now, that of the accused who would destroy his accuser, the ruthless man who was innocent and was made strong by that innocence.

"Say it now," Kane told him. "When we have a meeting of the Brotherhood, I'll have my say."

"All right." Kirby nodded. "I learned nothing important on this trip. I almost froze to death, and there were many times when I couldn't travel, but I found all the men you sent me to see. They believe the sentiment is about fifty-fifty. None of them would make a guess as to how many would fight if it came to that. When I was in South Park, the news that Fort Sumter had been fired on had not reached us."

"That's all?"

"That's all." Kirby hesitated, wanting to accuse Kane

of sending him on a wild-goose chase for private and selfish reasons. "The first thing I want to say is that Suzy and me are getting married in a few days. This time you will not stop it by sending me away."

"Are you saying you'll defy me?" Kane asked.

"No. I'm telling you how it is with us. Nothing in the oath I took in Kansas forces me to obey orders that interfere with my private life."

"I'll leave that for the Brotherhood to decide," Kane said stiffly, his eyes still narrowed, his lips still drawn tightly against his teeth. "There will be an assemblage soon because it's time to go to work. I have orders for you now. You are my best courier to Boulder and Gold Hill because you know Henry Elliot and Tony Harms. Tell them to be here at my cabin Saturday night by six o'clock. Randy"—he nodded at Curl—"will go to Golden City and the Gregory diggings. We simply can't wait, Grant. If you defy my order so that you can carry out your marriage plans, then by God, I promise you a firing squad the same as any disobedient soldier faces."

Kirby saw the familiar glitter in the narrowed eyes, the glitter he had not been sure he could identify, but now he thought he could. An illusion of greatness had grown in Martin Kane until he was a fanatic of the order of John Brown, and for that reason he was an equally dangerous man. Kirby wasn't sure he could prove it before an assemblage of the Brotherhood, but he had to try. Martin Kane had to be removed.

"When do I start?" Kirby said.

"Now," Kane answered. "We will have an assemblage Saturday night. Even that may be too late. I didn't realize until I saw the rebel flag this morning that we may have waited too long already."

Kirby had no idea what Kane's move would be, and he knew there was no sense in asking because his question would not be answered. He glanced at Randy Curl, who was obviously relieved that Kirby was taking Kane's orders.

"I'll get my horse," Kirby said, and, turning, strode back to E Street and followed Cherry Creek downstream to the Elephant Corral where he kept his buckskin.

TWENTY-FIVE

KIRBY had spent the night with Henry Elliot in Boulder and had left before daybreak, anxious to see Tony Harms in Gold Hill and get back to Denver. Suzy would have the time she needed, and he hoped she would be ready to marry him when he returned. As he rode through the chilly April dawn, he could not keep from smiling when he remembered Henry Elliot grumbling about being called to Denver for a meeting of the Brotherhood.

"We ain't had an assemblage for a hell of a long time," Elliot muttered. "I don't see why we have to have one now. Another day and you'd have missed me. I was aiming to leave in the morning and do some prospecting up Left Hand Creek."

"Martin Kane is not in the habit of taking me into his confidence," Kirby said, "but I got the notion after the flag business over the Wallingford and Murphy store that Kane figures on making a move of his own. Either that or he's afraid Dave Thorn's going to make one. I'm not sure which."

"Time and tide wait for no man," Elliot said darkly. "Wars don't neither, I reckon. Well, there's nothing to do but go. I took an oath, and now I'll be jumping to Martin Kane's tune whether I like it or not."

Tony Harms would say the same thing, Kirby thought, and he wondered how Randy Curl would come out with the men in Golden City and the Gregory diggings. Now that spring was here and active mining was starting again, he had a hunch that some of the men Kane was counting on would forget about their oaths or maybe be gone before Curl arrived.

Kirby turned up Four Mile Creek from the Boulder, studying the canyon walls on both sides of him and wondering if he would ever know enough about gold to be a prospector. For all he knew right now he might be riding beside a vein worth a million dollars. He glanced ahead at a cliff that jutted out of the side of the mountain, the road that followed the stream making a wide swing around it, and saw what looked like a bundle of rags in the dust. A moment later he realized it was a woman.

He spurred the buckskin, thinking of Laurie and hoping it wasn't she. He had worried about the girl a good deal during the winter, often wondering if he should have asked other people besides Tony Harms about her and Duke Rome. He always decided he had done the only thing he could, that he had no business interfering any more than he had.

He reined up beside the woman and stepped down. He knelt beside her and turned her over. It was Laurie.

Painfully thin, very pale, her dress faded and torn, her breath ragged, but it was Laurie.

He picked her up, shocked when he discovered how light she was. She was desperately sick, he thought, and he wondered what could possibly have driven her from her home. She must have walked all the way from her cabin the way her shoes looked.

"Laurie," he said as he put her down beside the creek. "Laurie, can you hear me?"

She made no response. He dipped water into his hat, and sloshed it on her face. He said, "Laurie, it's Kirby. Don't you know me?"

Her eyelids fluttered and opened and a tiny smile tugged at the corners of her mouth. "Kirby? Am I dead? Are we angels together?"

"We're not dead," he said. "Not by a jugful. Why are you here like this?"

"He's coming to kill you, Kirby." Her voice was so low he had to bend down to hear her. "Will you kiss me, Kirby? I wouldn't blame you if you wouldn't. You told me not to marry him. I wish I'd listened to you."

He bent down and kissed her. The smile came again. "I love you, Kirby. I guess it's all right for a woman to tell a man that if she's dying."

"You're not dying, Laurie," he said. "I'll get you to Boulder and find a doctor—"

"No." She lifted a hand and found his and squeezed it. "I've had this pain in my chest for a long time, Kirby. I ran and ran last night because I had to find you. I thought I'd have to go to Denver. I didn't think I'd find you on the road."

"I was going to Gold Hill to see Tony Harms again," Kirby told her.

"Listen to me, Kirby." She squeezed his hand again. "Al McCoy came to see Duke yesterday. He hired Duke to kill you. Duke thinks it's funny to get paid for something he wanted to do all the time. He's coming now. I heard his horse a while ago. He's hunting me, maybe. Or else he's on his way to Denver to find you."

She paused, her eyes closed. Every breath she took seemed to be a great effort. He said, "I'm going to take you to Boulder. We'll find a doctor—"

"No, Kirby," she whispered, her eyes coming open. "It's no use. I don't mind dying. I haven't anything to live for. It's been a nightmare all winter. I've had this pain, but Duke didn't think I was sick. He wouldn't get a doctor. I guess he didn't have any money to pay for one." She closed her eyes again, and she sounded very tired when she added, "I was too proud to go with you that time you told me you'd take me away. I didn't want to admit to you that I shouldn't have married him."

Again she stopped. He stared at her pale face, feeling sorry for her and at the same time hating Duke Rome as he had never hated another man in his life.

"Duke told the other men it would be a pleasure to kill you," she whispered, her eyes not opening this time. "He said he'd always hated you because you could beat him at everything you did, but he pretended to be your friend and you were stupid enough to think he was. He said that if McCoy and Thorn killed you, somebody might trace it to them, but nobody would suspect him. He told the other men to swear he'd never left Gold

Hill. He was drunk when he came to bed last night. Soon as he was asleep, I dressed and left the cabin. I had to find you and warn you. You're the only friend I ever had, Kirby. I ran and ran and fell down, and then I ran some more until I couldn't run any more. I just couldn't . . . run . . . any . . . more."

Her hand slipped out of his and fell back on her breast; the hint of a smile that had been on her mouth faded. Laurie Riley was gone, Laurie who had never had a chance at a decent life from the day she was born.

Carefully he lifted her, a wild and unreasoning anger soaring through him. Duke Rome had murdered this girl as effectually as if he had shot her through the head. Kirby would take her to Boulder, then he'd go on to Gold Hill, and after he saw Tony Harms, he'd look for Duke. . . .

"Put her down," Duke Rome said.

Kirby glanced up. Duke had left his horse where the road and creek made a sharp turn upstream around the cliff. He had his revolver in his hand. Standing with Laurie's lifeless body in his arms, Kirby knew that the instant he laid her down, Duke Rome would kill him. His intention was easy to read in his eyes, in the triumphant curl of his lips. Duke did not have the courage to face him in a fair fight. Oddly enough, he wondered in this strained moment how Duke had planned to kill him.

"She's dead, Duke," Kirby said.

"She was of some use when she was alive," Duke said. "She was a hell of a good cook. I guess I'll miss her, but if she'd stayed home where she belonged, she'd have been all right."

"You killed her," Kirby said. "I told her not to marry you."

"I know," Duke said, grinning a little. "Yes, sir, I know. She told me right after we were married, but now I'll tell you something, Mr. Know-It-All Grant. She was in love with you all the time, but I got her."

Staring at this man who faced him, Kirby wondered why he had ever thought of him as a friend. He wondered, too, why he had once thought Duke Rome had some human decency in him. Maybe he'd had a few good qualities when he'd lived in Kansas, and maybe Suzy was right when she said that Colorado brought out the worst in a man. Something had certainly brought the worst out in Duke Rome.

"Laurie told me you were hired to kill me," Kirby said.

"That's right, but I thought I'd have to go to Denver to earn my pay." Duke laughed nervously. "I'm guessing things are about to pop and maybe they were afraid you were smart enough to stop them. Now put her down, damn it."

Still Kirby held the body in his arms, considered the distance from his right hand, which was under Laurie's shoulders, to his holstered revolver. He wouldn't have any chance even if he dropped her and tried to pull his pistol and fire. Not now, facing Duke who had his gun in his hand.

"You can wait to earn your blood money," he said. "Let's take Laurie into town. Then we'll settle this."

"I'll take her into town after we settle it," Duke said. "I hate like hell to mess her body up, but if you won't put her down, I'm going to start shooting."

"Well, by God, you can wait ten seconds till I put her down on the grass yonder," Kirby said angrily.

He boldly turned his back on Duke and took three steps toward a grassy bench that lay between the creek and the road, but he didn't wait until he reached it. He dropped Laurie's body and sprawled on the ground and rolled over, clawing for his gun.

Duke, fooled for a second or two, didn't fire until Kirby hit the ground, then he let go, his first shot a clean miss, the second clipping hair off the back of Kirby's neck as he rolled over. The third sliced through the flesh of his right arm, a shallow wound that stung and bled profusely.

Duke had those three chances and no more, for Kirby had his gun in his hand then and pulled the trigger, the bullet hammering Duke in the chest and knocking him back on his heels so that his fourth shot was ten feet over Kirby's head. Kirby's second bullet struck him just above the nose and angled upward through his brain. He was dead by the time he hit the ground.

Kirby rose and for a moment stood looking down at Duke Rome's body, thinking that no amount of revenge could restore Laurie to life. She had loved him, and he had not known. Suzy had known it, though, and he pondered that. She had been jealous, and he'd thought she was crazy, but her woman's intuition had been right. He turned away as he holstered his gun, thinking how bad luck dogs some people as long as they live. That had been the story of Laurie's life.

Kirby left Duke's body beside the road, knowing it would soon be found and taken care of. He took Laurie into Boulder, then rode back to Henry Elliot's cabin and asked him to take Martin Kane's message to Tony Harms in Gold Hill. He told Elliot what he had done, and said he'd thought about seeing the marshal and telling him what had happened, but Elliot reminded him that the marshal was friendly with the secesh crowd. He'd remember that Kirby had shot John Deal, and he'd use Duke Rome's killing to hang Kirby.

"You hike on back to Denver," Elliot said, "and let sleeping dogs lie. Long as nobody saw what happened, just play innocent and they won't hook you up with Rome's killing. We've got too much to do to fight a murder trial."

"I guess you're right," Kirby said.

He rode to Denver that afternoon. Two days later Laurie was buried in a cemetery south of town. When they were back in Suzy's cabin, Kirby told her that Laurie had left Gold Hill to save his life and had used up what strength she had running to find him.

Suddenly Suzy began to cry. She dabbed at her eyes, then she said vehemently, "I hate myself, Kirby. I knew she loved you and I knew she needed you. She was like a child, so damned helpless. When I was in my right mind, I knew I had no reason to be jealous because I was sure you loved me. I should have made you get her and bring her to Denver where I could have taken care of her."

"No," Kirby said thoughtfully. "I've asked myself about this ever since it happened. She never had been happy. Maybe she couldn't be because she didn't know how. Anyhow, I don't think it would have changed her luck if you had brought her here. I doubt that she really wanted to live."

"You may be right," Suzy said, "but I should have tried, for my sake if not for hers."

TWENTY-SIX

KIRBY intended to sleep late Saturday morning, but he was jarred awake before sunup by an insistent knocking on his door at the Broadwell House. He crossed the room, knuckling his eyes and yawning as he mentally cursed the man who was hammering on his door.

He opened the door a crack, thinking of a few choice words which would express his feelings to the man in the hall, but he didn't use any of them. Bill Jones stood there, an impatient expression on his face. "You and Suzy must have had a night," Bill said as he pushed past Kirby into the room. "I've been skinning my knuckles on your door for the last five minutes."

Kirby yawned loudly and sat down on the bed. "I'm going to marry the girl," he said, "in case you've got a shotgun behind your back. We're planning to get the job done tomorrow."

"Oh, hell," Bill said in disgust. "I don't care if you marry her or not. She's a big girl and she can look out for herself. I came for you. Put your clothes on and fetch your rifle and your six-shooter. We've got work to do."

Angry, Kirby said, "I won't do it. My life has been a series of monotonous events. Suzy and I set a time to get married, and Kane keeps us from it. I won't let it happen this time."

"You'll let it happen, all right," Bill said sharply. "You took an oath, and this time it applies. Now will you get a move on?"

Kirby regarded Bill gravely for a moment, then he said, "I reckon I'm the one who'll decide if my oath applies or not."

"All right, decide it," Bill snapped, "and then get dressed, or do I report you to Kane as a deserter?"

"So you two and Randy Curl can try me and decide to execute me like you did Archibald Bland?" Kirby rose and reached for his shirt. "You know what I think, Bill? I think Martin Kane is a coward, but he's crazy for power. He uses good men like you and Curl, but he never seems to do the dangerous jobs himself. Sure, he'll shoot Archibald Bland in the back of his head when he's helpless, but you put a gun in Bland's hand and see what happens."

Bill didn't say a word until Kirby had finished dressing and was buckling a gun belt around his waist. Then he said slowly and thoughtfully, "I haven't admitted it even to Suzy, but you're right. He's changed since I came to Denver. I've known it for quite a while. Once we get a loyal governor out here, we won't need Kane, but we don't have one yet, so Kane is the only man in a position to lead us. It may be hard to keep him from going hog wild, but we can do it."

Kirby picked up his rifle. "You're saying you wouldn't back Kane if it comes to a showdown between him and me, for instance?"

"I wouldn't say right now what I'd do," Bill said, "but

if it came to a showdown between him and you, I wouldn't stand for another execution like I did with Arch Bland."

"What about Randy Curl?"

Bill spread his hands in a gesture of futility. "Randy's got the kind of loyalty that would make him shoot his own mother if Kane told him it had to be done. We've got a couple more men here in Denver who are the same. What about the men in Boulder and Gold Hill? And the Gregory diggings? You met all of them last fall."

"I can't answer for all of them," Kirby said, "but I'm sure about Henry Elliot. He won't take Kane's orders blindly." He put his hat on and moved to the door. "Do you think Kane will try to grab power before the governor gets here?"

"He might," Bill admitted. "I've gone along with everything he wanted so far because I thought I had to, but like I said, he's been changed by what's happened. He gets more arrogant, more sure of himself all the time—and he hates you."

"Why?"

Bill shrugged. "Maybe he's after—I've wondered about that. But it's more likely he can't stand defiance, and you've been tough for him to handle. You're too much inclined to think for yourself."

They followed Larimer Street for a block, then turned down F Street. Kirby asked, "Where are we going?"

"We'll get our horses out of the Elephant Corral," Bill answered. "By that time Suzy will have breakfast ready for us. Then we'll go to Kane's cabin. Randy Curl's with him. Another man should be there by the time we are, a

Kansas man named Phil Norton. He's like Curl, a Kane man all the way."

Kirby walked in silence for a time, thinking this was a hell of a situation. To believe in something, to be willing to die for it was one thing, but to be badly led was another. A man deserved the leadership of someone even more dedicated than he was, someone who would not change with time and events to become more arrogant and sure of himself as Bill admitted Martin Kane had.

For a moment the temptation to walk away from this whole business was almost overpowering in Kirby. The oath he had taken in Kansas should not be binding now. He had never sworn to follow a man like Martin Kane.

"You haven't told me what's going on," Kirby said after a time. "Is it a secret?"

Bill glanced obliquely at him, hesitating, then he said, "You've got your neck bowed, son. Maybe you've got a right to, but don't start a fight among ourselves. This ain't the time."

"I was put to work right after I got to Colorado," Kirby said, irritation growing in him. "My personal life has been interfered with at the whim of a man I do not respect, and still I have never been permitted to come to an assemblage, I have not met the other Denver members, and now if I'm expected to go out and fight and maybe get killed, I aim to know what's going on."

"It's fair enough." Bill smiled wryly. "I know how you feel. In fact, I mentioned it to Kane, but he said he was afraid you'd create friction if you attended an assemblage."

"I figured to create a hell of a lot of friction tonight,"

Kirby said grimly, "and I was coming whether Kane liked it or not."

"He aimed for you to be there tonight," Bill said. "Personally I'm glad you're not, because it would have meant trouble which we can't afford right now." He hesitated, then added, "I'm not supposed to tell you, but I will, and you can look surprised when Kane tells us. Randy Curl got back from the Gregory diggings in time to take a turn at watching Dave Thorn's barn. Before midnight Thorn and McCoy drove their horse herd out of town. Randy brought the word to Kane, and Phil Norton followed the herd."

"I don't know that it means anything," Kirby said thoughtfully.

"Sure it does," Bill said. "They took the horses up the Platte. We've heard Thorn had the percussion caps hidden up there somewhere. We've also heard that a band of rebels have been getting together up the river to drill."

Suddenly Kirby remembered the rumor that Thorn had brought the horses out here to mount a band of rebel cavalry. Yes, Bill must be right. This was no time for his personal problems, no time to buck Martin Kane. Thorn had to be stopped before the horses were delivered to the men who were waiting for them up the Platte.

They saddled their horses and rode to the Jones cabin where Suzy had breakfast for them. She had been crying, Kirby saw, and when they finished eating and were ready to go, she threw herself into Kirby's arms.

"Don't go, darling," she cried. "Please don't go."

"We're soldiers in an army," he said. "Remember?"

She drew her head back to look at him, her lips quivering. Then she said, "Kirby, I'd be the last person on earth to ask you to do less than your duty. This is war even if there are no bands playing and no flags waving, but I don't like Martin Kane giving the orders. He'll keep you from coming back if he can."

"Now wait a minute, Sis," Bill said. "I've got my doubts about Martin the same as Kirby has, but you're going too far."

She shook her head. "Remember the story of David in the Bible, about Uriah and Bathsheba?"

"Sure," Bill said. "David sent Uriah out to be killed so he could marry the widow, but Martin wouldn't—" He stopped and stared at his sister. "Are you trying to say Kane would do that?"

"He certainly would," Suzy said. "He's been here several times when you were gone. I didn't tell either of you because I thought it would make trouble, and there wasn't anything you could do. Maybe you can't now, but I had to tell you."

"You're sure you know what you're saying?" Bill asked.

She nodded. "He asked me to marry him. He's promised me the moon when this is over and he's the big man in the territory. The last time when I turned him down and said I was going to marry Kirby, he got so mad he was kind of crazy. He told me he'd see to it I didn't marry Kirby, and stomped out."

"We'll keep our eyes open," Kirby said. "Don't worry. If I don't come back, it will be because I have Dave Thorn's bullet in me, not Martin Kane's."

Bill nodded. "I'll be giving the orders for a while. Martin's staying in Denver while the rest of us chase the horses." He jerked his head at Kirby. "If we don't get over there to his cabin, he'll kill both of us."

Kirby kissed Suzy and held her in his arms long enough to whisper, "I'm coming back in one piece and then I'm going to marry you."

"I wonder if that day will ever come," she answered, and tried to smile.

"Sure it will," he said, and turned quickly from her.

He followed Bill outside to the horses. He mounted, made a farewell gesture to Suzy, and rode away. Maybe it would be easier, he thought, if he were in uniform, with flags waving and the bands playing.

Two horses were tied in front of Kane's cabin. Curl's and Norton's, Kirby guessed, and thought that what Bill had said about Kane staying here today while the rest of them chased horses was proof of what he suspected about Martin Kane, that the man was a coward, but he was skilled at using other men to achieve his ends. In one day he was receiving proof of too many things he had suspected about Kane.

Kane scowled when Kirby and Bill stepped into the cabin. "Where the hell have you two been? You knew there was great need of haste, but you've been—"

"Martin," Bill said, "You're the leader and you're giving the orders and we're taking them, so get on with it."

Kane stopped, his face turning red. For a time his breathing was the only sound in the room. He was not used to being talked to this way, and certainly not by Bill

Jones. Then he recovered his self-possession and said, "All right." He nodded at a red-faced man who was a stranger to Kirby. "Phil trailed the horse herd until about dawn. When he started back, Thorn and McCoy were letting the horses graze. The two men were eating breakfast, and will probably sleep awhile. We have no way of knowing how far they'll take the horses, but they'll go slow because they won't want to tire the animals out so much the men can't ride hard when the time comes."

Kane went on thoughtfully, "We don't know for sure how far away the men are who will ride them, although I have information that indicates they are somewhere near Pueblo in the mountains. All I can say now is that your job is to catch the horses before they reach their destination. Any questions?"

"We may be gone quite a while," Bill said. "What about grub?"

Kane motioned toward four partly filled sacks on the floor. "I've fixed enough grub in each sack to last a couple of days or more. I expect to catch up with you sometime tonight or tomorrow at the latest. I'll have the rest of our brothers who will gather here for the assemblage. I'll bring the pack horses."

"Suppose we catch up with the outfit that Thorn expects to meet?" Randy Curl asked.

"Your job is to keep the horses from falling into their hands," Kane said. "How you do it will be up to you. Bill is in command until I get there. I expect to have eight men with me. That will make twelve with you four. If we have to tackle the entire rebel company, we'll do it." He motioned to the sacks of food. "Take the grub and get started."

They filed out, each man picking up a sack and tying it behind his saddle. Kirby turned to Norton and held out his hand. "I'm Kirby Grant. I take it you're Phil Norton."

"You take it right," Norton said, shaking hands.

"I've got a question," Kirby said. "Did Thorn or McCoy have any idea you were trailing them?"

"They sure as hell didn't," Norton said as if insulted.

"Good," Kirby said and, turning to his buckskin, stepped into the saddle.

They rode south, Bill in the lead. All need of concealment was gone now. If any of the Criterion crowd was watching, they would know Bill Jones's identity. Probably Martin Kane's, too. Then, suddenly and without apparent cause, a thought rocked Kirby. Could it be possible that Martin Kane, and not Dave Thorn, had sent McCoy to hire Duke Rome to murder him? He tried to put the thought out of his mind, but it still lingered, spreading its lethal poison.

TWENTY-SEVEN

WITHIN the hour they were following the tracks of the horse herd. Shortly after noon they reached the place where Norton had left them. Apparently they had remained here several hours, resting the riders and the horses. Norton rode on up the river about fifty yards, then stepped out of the saddle and knelt on the ground to study the tracks. He mounted and rode back to where the other three men waited.

"They're moving pretty fast," Norton said thoughtfully. "They ain't been gone more'n an hour, I'd say."

"They stayed here quite a while," Bill said, "so it looks to me like they figured all they had to do to be safe was to get the horses out of town without being seen."

"It's the things we don't know that's bothering me," Kirby said. "We don't know how far they aim to go tonight, we don't know how far away the rebels are who're going to ride these horses, and we don't know how much they know about us."

Bill nodded thoughtfully, then turned to Norton. "Got any notion how far they'll go tonight? You know the country better'n the rest of us."

Norton nodded. "I've got a notion, all right, but it sure as hell might be wrong."

"Well, let's have it," Bill said impatiently.

"A feller named Brooks used to have a purty good business fetching horses and mules to Denver from New Mexico," Norton said. "That was when the town was first started and men were coming in on foot and others had lost their horses or mules on the trail. He built a string of corrals along the foothills south of here. The closest one to Denver is just up the river a piece on the other side. It's down in a kind of holler with some pines scattered around. It sure ain't much for a man to fight from, but I reckon Brooks didn't aim to do no fighting. Thorn and McCoy don't, either, if I'm guessing right."

"You figure Thorn and McCoy will throw the herd into the corral and stay there all night?" Bill asked.

Norton shrugged. "It's just a guess, but looks like they let the horses graze here. They wouldn't have done that if they had a notion anybody was on their tail. The corral I'm talking about is big enough for thirty-five head, which is about what Thorn's got, and it'd be a place they wouldn't be straying from."

"If they don't figure on being chased," Randy Curl said, "they won't be in a hurry."

"How far is it to this corral?" Bill asked Norton.

"Oh, maybe two hours' ride for us," Norton said. "Be longer for them, seeing as they can't push them horses as fast as we'll be riding." He cocked his head and glanced at the sun. "If we don't stop to cook dinner, I'm guessing they won't beat us there by much. Might be we'll catch up with 'em before they get there."

"We won't make a dinner stop," Bill said. "Let's get moving."

He led out, the others following. Half an hour later they forded the river, the tracks leading to a bench on the west side. Far ahead they saw a cloud of dust, and Norton nodded in satisfaction. He said, "I told you I figured we'd catch 'em."

"You say the corral is down in a hollow?" Bill asked.

"Kind of," Norton said. "Leastwise there's a ridge on this side. I ain't been there for a spell, but that's the way I remember it. Seems to me there was a cabin up the slope a piece from the corral."

Bill nodded, and Kirby, glancing at him, wondered if the same thought was in Bill's mind that was in his. The thing to do was to let Thorn and McCoy reach the corral. If it was in a hollow, it should be easy enough to capture both men, or kill them from the rim if they resisted.

But it wasn't quite that simple. An hour and a half later

Norton told them the corral was only a quarter of a mile away. Dismounting shortly after that, they left their horses and moved on foot to the rim which really wasn't a rim at all, but simply a breaking off of the bench they had been following.

They lay belly flat, looking at the corral below them, a cabin upslope about fifty feet from it. Two other men had been waiting here, or had joined Thorn and McCoy on the trail. McCoy and two strangers were watering the horses. As Kirby and the others watched, the three men herded the horses into the corral, and Thorn, who apparently had been building a fire inside the cabin, came out and started chopping wood from a deadfall that lay between the cabin and a ravine that cut down the slope and ran on to the river.

"Well, what are we waiting for?" Randy Curl asked impatiently. "Let's get 'em. It'll be like shooting sitting ducks."

It would be like him, Kirby thought, and certainly like Martin Kane if he were here, but Kirby couldn't do it. Before he remembered that it was Bill Jones's place to say yes or no, he blurted, "No."

Bill looked at him. He asked sharply, "You taking over, Kirby?"

"I'm sorry." Kirby shook his head. "I'm not trying to take over, Bill, but it was such a damn fool thing for Curl to say."

"Why?" Bill asked. "These men are rebels. Traitors. Maybe they're a cut above Charley Harrison and the Criterion crowd, but they're the same breed of dogs. I risked my life all winter hanging around that damned hell hole trying to pick up some information. If they'd got onto me, Dave Thorn or any of 'em, I'd have had my hide ventilated with lead before I could have yelled 'Hurray for Jefferson Davis.'"

"I know," Kirby said.

For a moment Kirby was silent, knowing that his sentimental feeling about Dave Thorn would not be understood by Bill or either of the others. Maybe it was ridiculous. Certainly there was no sense trying to tell them about it, but it was so strong that he would have pulled his gun on his friends before he would have allowed these men to be shot down in cold blood.

"Well then," Bill said, "if you know, why was it a damned fool thing for Randy to say? Right now we can get 'em. Five minutes from now maybe we can't."

"We can still get 'em," Kirby said. "They're not going anywhere. I say it's a fool thing to cut 'em down from here without giving 'em a chance to talk. They know things we need to know, so let's take 'em prisoner."

"Oh, hell," Curl said. "You won't get anything out of men like that. They'd swing before they'd tell anything they knew."

"Then we can swing 'em," Kirby said. "I can tell you one thing. Martin Kane will cuss us good if we smoke these men down and don't learn anything."

He didn't believe this, for Kane's sole purpose was to prevent Thorn's horses from being delivered to the rebels who were waiting for them. Kirby was certain that if Kane were here, he'd say to shoot the four men down without giving them a chance, but Bill believed him. Even Curl and Norton gave it some thought.

"All right," Bill said finally. "What do you suggest?"

Kirby motioned to the ravine that ran downslope just a little west of the cabin before it angled toward the river. "Give me two minutes," he said. "I'll get down there close enough to talk to Thorn, then you cut loose at the other three if you want to."

"Two minutes," Bill said. "No more."

McCoy and the two strangers were grouped in front of the corral gate talking, and Thorn was still cutting wood when Kirby slipped off the ridgetop into the ravine. He moved as fast as he could through the brush, making more noise than he intended, and all the time he was asking himself why he felt as he did about Dave Thorn, a man who was fully as dedicated to taking Colorado Territory into the Confederacy as Martin Kane was in keeping it in the Union, a man who had sent McCoy to Gold Hill to hire Duke Rome to murder him, and who before that had probably sent John Deal to Boulder on the same errand.

He had no answer and little time to seek one. He climbed out of the ravine when he judged he was opposite where Thorn was cutting wood. He heard the rhythmical chunk-chunk of the ax as it bit into the hard body of the pine. His gun was in his hand when he climbed out of the ravine.

He found himself closer to Thorn than he had expected, not more than twenty feet, but Thorn was so preoccupied with his woodchopping that he had no hint Kirby was there until he called, "Put your hands up, Dave."

Thorn dropped his ax and spun around just as rifle fire

broke out from the rim. For a second Thorn's face was filled with dismay. He must have known instantly that this was final and complete disaster. He didn't run or say a word or put up his hands. In that brief interval of time he apparently made a decision to die rather than surrender, for his hand swept downward to his gun and he lifted it from the holster.

"No, Dave," Kirby yelled. "Don't make me kill you."

There seemed to be no expression on Thorn's strong, square face. He was a soldier facing death, no more, no less, and Kirby, who had risked his life in an effort to save the life of this man who had once been his friend, knew Thorn would kill him if he could. He pulled the trigger; he heard the deafening sound of the gun and saw the burst of smoke, then it drifted away. Thorn stood there, his right arm hanging limply at his side, his gun on the ground.

The firing from the rim had died, and Bill, Curl and Norton were pounding down the slope, Bill shouting, "You all right, Kirby?"

"I'm all right," Kirby called.

Blood dripped from Thorn's right hand. He said, "You should have killed me, Kirby. They'll hang me now, and you won't want to see that. I chose to die with your bullet in me, but all I've got is a broken arm."

Kirby had not thought of that before, but he realized Thorn was right. Martin Kane would be here sometime tonight after the danger was over, and he would hang Dave Thorn as surely as the sun would come up in the morning.

"I couldn't," Kirby said, "but you would have killed

me if I hadn't fired."

"Yes," Thorn said. "I would have killed you. It's important that I live, and I'd have had a chance if I'd got you."

"Why did you send McCoy to Gold Hill to hire Duke Rome to murder me?" Kirby asked.

Thorn hesitated. "I didn't. I've considered having you killed more than once because I've been afraid of you ever since you quit working for me, but you weren't in Denver very much, so I didn't figure you were hurting us."

He had moved back to lean against the cabin wall, his face going pale. Blood dripped steadily down his arm. Kirby stepped forward and picked up his gun. Just as Bill came around the corner of the cabin, Dave Thorn spilled forward in a faint.

"He's not dead," Kirby said. "I busted his shooting arm. He's losing some blood, but I guess you can stop it."

Taking his knife from his pocket, Bill slit Thorn's sleeve all the way down from the shoulder. He nodded as he said, "He'll live long enough to taste a rope."

"What about the others?"

"Two of 'em are dead. McCoy's alive, but he won't be around much longer."

"Is he able to talk?"

"He's able, but he's not a mind to. Here, help me. . . ."

But Kirby was already around the cabin and going toward the corral in a dead run. McCoy lay on his back not far from the corral gate. Curl and Norton stood over him, Curl with his gun in his hand. "Damn it, you'd better loosen your tongue or I'll let you have it again," Curl was saying. "Where are those percussion caps?"

Even with death only seconds away, Al McCoy was not going to talk. Blood bubbled from the corners of his mouth and ran down his chin. He raised a hand and wiped it away as he muttered, "Go to hell."

Kirby was there then, shoving Curl's gun barrel to one side. "I've got a question to ask that maybe he'll answer. Who hired you to pay Duke Rome to kill me?"

The dying man's eyes moved just enough to stare at Kirby. A sardonic smile was on his lips as he said, "Martin Kane."

For an instant Curl and Norton were too shocked to speak or move, then Curl began to curse. He yelled, "You're a goddamned liar," and kicked McCoy viciously in the ribs, but McCoy didn't feel it. His lips had parted; his eyes had lost their defiance and now held only the blankness of death.

Curl whirled on Kirby, shouting, "Martin wouldn't do that. You know he wouldn't, Kirby."

Norton nodded. "That's right, Kirby. McCoy was lying."

"A dying man doesn't lie," Kirby said as he turned away.

TWENTY-EIGHT

KIRBY sat on a bench inside the cabin, his gaze on Dave Thorn who lay on the bunk. Dave's arm was hurting him, Kirby knew, but they had nothing to give him except some whiskey from a bottle they found in the cabin. Apparently Thorn and his men had used the cabin before because he had told Kirby where to find the bottle.

Randy Curl had ridden back toward Denver to intercept Martin Kane and his party and bring them here. Bill Jones and Phil Norton were outside. Thorn had refused to answer any questions except the one about where the men were waiting for the horses. A combination of fury and frustration had made him blurt out, "On the other side of Pueblo, damn it. Too far from here to help me." Then he seemed to regret saying that much. He shut his mouth tightly and would say nothing more.

Threats of instant death or of slow torture had not brought another word from Thorn. Finally, when he had refused for the tenth time to tell where the percussion caps were hidden, Randy Curl said, "By God, Thorn, you'll talk when Martin Kane gets here. I'll bet on it."

After Curl left, Thorn said, "Kane will use every trick in the book to make me talk, Kirby. Think you can stand there and watch it?"

"No, I don't think I can," Kirby said. "I've got a score to settle with Kane. Maybe that will be the time to settle it."

"With a dozen men on his side?" Thorn shook his head. "I doubt that you will, Kirby."

That had been more than an hour ago, and Kirby had been thinking about it ever since. Once he stepped out of the cabin and told Bill what Al McCoy had said just before he'd died. Bill said, "Well, he lied, Kirby. There are a lot of things about Martin Kane I don't like, but he doesn't operate that way. He may decide you've got to die, but if he does, he'll handle it the way he handled Archibald Bland."

"You think it was Thorn?"

"Sure it was Thorn," Bill said. "They tried to get Duke Rome to do it so there would be no way to connect them with it. Naturally it never occurred to them that Laurie would see McCoy or hear the talk and warn you."

Kirby returned to his seat in the cabin and stared at Dave Thorn, pale-faced, teeth gritted to hold back the groans, a strong man now physically weak. Kirby kept telling himself it was war, that under these circumstances a man lies just as he kills and steals and burns so his side will win. McCoy had known he was dying. Still, he had lied because he thought it would make trouble between Kirby and Kane. Thorn would lie, too. It was stupid even to consider the possibility that he would admit to Kirby that he had hired a man to murder him.

Kirby told himself that under those circumstances he would lie, too, dying or not. Martin Kane would not waste money hiring a killer. Even if he did, he would not use Al McCoy, a known enemy, to be the go-between. But it was water over the dam. What worried Kirby now was Kane's action when he arrived with the other men. Would they hang Thorn as Thorn was so certain they would?

Suddenly Thorn turned on his good shoulder and faced Kirby. He asked, "What are you thinking about, boy?"

"Traitors," Kirby said. "Spies. Secret societies. If Congress had organized the territory sooner and sent a governor out here, maybe all this wouldn't be happening."

"No," Thorn said. "You're wrong about that. Kansas

was an organized territory and had one governor after another. Even some federal troops were there, but we still had secret societies, don't forget, and murders and stealings and burnings. It's the natural way for a war like this to be fought where men are worked up over an issue so much that death is better than letting the other side win."

It was almost dark now, with only a rosy hint in the sky that the sun had set behind the western peaks. Kirby rose and lighted the candle that was on the table and sat down again. He said, "Why didn't you tell me how you felt when we crossed the Plains? I didn't make any secret about how I felt."

"My usefulness depended on people not knowing my feelings," Thorn said. "It was the same with several of us. Kane, for instance. And Bill Jones. He was the smartest. He drank and played cards in the Criterion all winter, and made everybody think he was on our side. He's a hell of a good man, Jones is, but I can't say as much for your Martin Kane."

Kirby, staring at him in the thin light, thought, "He knows I've had trouble with Kane, so he's working on me." He remained silent, letting Thorn talk.

"That's the trouble with times like these," Thorn went on. "It's pretty hard to separate the men who honestly believe in their side from the ones who use a fight to fill their own pockets. It happened in Kansas. You know it as well as I do. Men stole horses for their profit as well as to hurt their enemies."

It was true. Kirby had seen it happen. He didn't have the slightest doubt about Martin Kane being that kind of man. He still wasn't sure Bill was right about Kane not hiring McCoy, but whether he was right or wrong, Kirby was dead sure that the differences between him and Kane would come to a head tonight.

"Remember a talk we had when you stayed with Liz and McCoy and the horses on Cherry Creek?" Thorn asked. "That last night before you got to Denver?"

"I remember," Kirby said.

"You remember we talked about the Vigilantes," Thorn said. "I told you there was an inner circle of ten men who decided the guilt of the man they were after, then they'd take him out and hang him."

"I remember the talk," Kirby said. "I've thought about it a good many times since then."

"After living in Denver all winter," Thorn went on, "and having spies out the same as your side, I still don't know who's on the committee of ten, but it could be your man Kane was and still is. He operates the same way, don't he? He'll ride in here after a while and they'll try me. They'll call it a trial, but it will be a farce, and you know it as well as I do because they've already decided to hang me. The so-called Vigilantes do exactly the same thing."

"I guess there isn't any doubt what you've done and what you were trying to do when we caught you," Kirby said.

"Can you prove it?" Thorn asked. "Can Kane prove it? Will he even try?" Thorn waved his good hand as if to thrust such questions to one side. "It's murder, Kirby. I have a right to be tried in a legal court with counsel. I have a right to have my guilt established by twelve men, and I have the right to have sentence pronounced on me by a legally appointed judge. You agree?"

"Of course I agree," Kirby said, "but do you expect me to stop Kane?"

"Yes, I do," Thorn said. "You and Bill Jones and anyone else in the crowd who believes in law and order. What are you really fighting for, you and Bill and the others?"

"The Union," Kirby said. "If the Union is broken, the nation is broken. We can't let it happen, Dave. That's why you're a traitor. If you have your way, you'd wreck what's taken almost a hundred years to build."

"A traitor," Thorn murmured. "An ugly word, boy. About the ugliest word in the English language. Maybe it never occurred to you that a man who would take away the Constitutional rights of a sovereign state is a traitor. Or has it ever occurred to you that you and your father were worse than horse thieves when you helped slaves escape? You were stealing valuable property, you know."

"I've never regretted any part I had in that," Kirby said thoughtfully, "although I know the argument as well as you do. No one, Dave Thorn or Jeff Davis or anyone else has a right to turn a human being into a piece of property."

"But it was legal," Thorn said. "You were the ones breaking the law the same as you will be if you hang me. It's murder, Kirby. You can't make anything else out of it."

Thorn stared at Kirby as he waited for Kirby to answer his argument. When Kirby let the silence run on, Thorn said. "Think of it another way, boy. Is the business about the Union half as important as law and order right here under your nose? What good is it to hold your precious Union together if a gang of murderers who call themselves Vigilantes or who belong to some secret society hang a man and go untouched by the law?"

Kirby rose. There was no logical answer to it. Dave Thorn was right. He could not answer Thorn's question. Of course the man was using Kirby as his last faint hope for life, but that had nothing to do with him being right or wrong. If the shoe was on the other foot, Thorn would not worry about law and order. Kirby Grant would be killed just as he could have been killed by Thorn today, or would have been killed on the road to Gold Hill if Laurie had not warned him about Duke Rome, or if Duke had been a tougher and faster man.

Kirby left the cabin as Thorn reached for the whiskey bottle. Outside the stars had appeared and the last of the dusk light had left the earth. The scattered pine trees resembled huge, black spears pointed at the sky. He hunkered in front of the fire as Bill threw more wood on it. He knew it wasn't any good to say to himself what Dave Thorn would do if the shoe was on the other foot. The question was what Kirby Grant was going to do.

Phil Norton appeared out of the shadows and warmed himself at the fire for a moment. He said worriedly, "I wish to hell we knew for sure that Thorn was telling the truth about their outfit being down around Pueblo."

"I figure he was," Bill said. "It ties in with something Martin heard. They've got a camp back in the mountains where they've been drilling, but now half of 'em will be on foot."

Norton grunted something, then he said, "Just the same, I'd better stay out there in the brush. It'd be hell if they surprised us."

He disappeared. Kirby, because he could not stand it any longer, told Bill what Thorn had said. "He's right," Kirby finished. "I want to marry Suzy and have a family and make my home here, but if my life isn't going to be safe, or if my property isn't safe—"

"Damn it, don't you see what the man's doing?" Bill demanded. "He's guilty, and he knows what's going to happen to him, so you're the one chance he's got. If you can stir up enough trouble—"

"I know that," Kirby broke in, "but it doesn't change anything. Guilty or not, he has a right to be taken to Denver and tried for treason."

Bill stared at him across the fire. Finally he said, "You're a hell of an honest man, Kirby. An idealist, I guess you'd say. Like your dad. Even men like John Brown and Colonel James Montgomery are, too, but there's times like this when you've got to forget about law. It won't work because it isn't here to work. Dave Thorn will swing from that pine limb yonder and there's nothing you or me can do to stop it."

Kirby looked down at the fire, knowing this was the day of judgment. Not for Dave Thorn who was a traitor in Kirby's eyes. The judgment was of Kirby Grant. Suppose he returned to Denver and married Suzy, and one night some men came into his house and accused him of stealing a horse, then they took him outside and lynched him?

Maybe one of those men wanted Suzy, and they knew

as well as he did that he had not stolen a horse. That man could be Martin Kane, using this trouble to cover his private and selfish ambition. Tonight Kirby Grant was on the winning side; tomorrow night he might not be, but there would be no law to protect him. You believe in law and order or you don't. It was that simple. He knew then what he must do.

TWENTY-NINE

SHORTLY after midnight Martin Kane and Randy Curl rode in, a dozen other horsemen strung out behind them. Kirby and Bill Jones had been dozing by the fire. Now they threw more wood on the coals. The blaze leaped up in flickering tongues, throwing an uncertain and shifting light into the darkness.

Martin Kane strode toward the fire, leaving Curl to take care of his horse. Staring at him in the firelight, Kirby thought that tonight Kane had a new role. He was the conqueror, the man who had sent a force ahead of him that had won a fight, and now he was here to occupy the conquered land and to try the prisoner of war.

Kane looked at Bill Jones. "Where's Thorn?"

"Inside the cabin."

"Norton?"

"He's down the trail a piece," Bill answered. "Thorn said the men who were waiting for the horses were at Pueblo, but Norton wasn't sure he was telling the truth, so he . . ."

"Thorn was," Kane said. "Bring Norton in."

Kane strode toward the cabin. Kirby caught up with him, Kane's superiority of manner and commanding tone honing his temper to a fine edge. He asked, "How do you know he's telling the truth?"

Kane turned on him. He said in a voice so low that only Kirby heard, "By God, Grant, I've stood all of your insolence and insubordination I'm going to. After we get done hanging Thorn, we'll try you and hang you right beside him."

There it was at last, as frank a statement of intention as Kirby could expect. He said, "I wish somebody else had heard that, Kane. I suppose you have to shut my mouth because the men you hired to kill me didn't get the job done."

Kane was shocked by surprise. He asked, "What men?"

"Duke Rome. Before him it was John Deal."

"I don't know any Duke Rome or John Deal, and I don't know what you're talking about," Kane snapped, and went on toward the cabin. When he saw that Kirby was coming with him, he stopped again, "I'll talk to Thorn privately."

"No," Kirby said. "Thorn has a right to a lawyer and I'm it."

"You appointed yourself?"

"That's right, but he'll take me, seeing as there isn't anyone else."

For a moment Kane stood motionless, staring at Kirby in the darkness, then he said sullenly, "I knew you were trouble when you showed up at the meeting the night Archibald Bland was tried. If it hadn't been for Suzy and

Bill, I'd have got rid of you before this."

"Because Suzy loves me?"

"That's as good a reason as any," Kane said, and would have gone on into the cabin if Kirby had not reached out and gripped his shoulder.

"Kane, you don't fool me a little bit," Kirby said. "Before the night's over, I'm going to expose you to every man here."

"You've got nothing to expose," Kane shot back. "I'm in command. If you think I'll have any trouble hanging you for disobeying your commanding officer, you're crazy. Now get your hand off my shoulder."

Kirby's hand tightened. "You're going to listen to me first. You've got plenty to expose. I don't know about John Deal, but you tried to have me murdered by Duke Rome. McCoy said it just before he died, and he knew he was dying. Thorn says that if he had decided they had to get rid of me, they would have done it themselves and not hired an outsider like Rome. And another thing. Before we left Denver, Suzy told Bill and me you'd been after her to marry you. I'd suspected it a long time, but I hadn't been sure. You sent me to South Park because you thought a blizzard would get me."

"That all?"

"Not quite. Kane, I'll give you credit for believing at one time in what we're doing, but not now. It just isn't important to you any more. There's nothing lower than a man who uses a good cause and a worthy organization to gain his own selfish ends, and that's what you're doing."

"We'll see who can prove what," Kane said. "We'll see."

He shook off Kirby's hand and went inside. Picking up the candle, he walked to the bunk and looked down at Thorn's pale, drawn face. For a time he didn't say anything, but stood there motionless, staring at the wounded man.

"I'm Martin Kane," he said finally. "I'm the Colorado commander of the Brotherhood of Free Soilers. You will be tried for high treason, Thorn."

"I wish I could do the same for you, Kane," Thorn said, "but the fortunes of war seem to have delivered me into your hands."

"That's right," Kane said with satisfaction. "We had one advantage. We knew who you were, but you didn't know who I was."

"The first skirmish does not mean the war," Thorn said. "There will be other battles. Right now Texas is raising a force to invade New Mexico. They'll come on north into Colorado. The Confederacy can't afford to lose the West."

"But it will." Kane jerked a thumb at Kirby. "Grant says he is your lawyer. That right?"

Thorn managed a grin. "Sure it's right."

Kirby thought he might as well have added that he knew it wouldn't do any good to have a lawyer, but he didn't. Kane said, "Can you walk, or do you want to be carried outside?"

"I'll walk," Thorn said, and put his feet on the floor and stood up.

"One more thing," Kane said. "I'll be in charge of the trial. I promise you that you would improve your position if you tell us where you hid the percussion caps."

"I don't have any percussion caps," Thorn said blandly.

"All right," Kane said. "Walk to the fire. I don't think this will take long."

Thorn made it through the door, then he stumbled and almost fell, and after that Kirby held to his arm. When they reached the fire, Kirby saw that Phil Norton had come in from his post and stood beside Bill Jones. The others formed a solid mass on the south side of the fire.

Kirby recognized Henry Elliot and Tony Harms and the men he had talked to in Golden City and the Gregory Gulch camps last fall. Some like Norton would side with Kane regardless of the issue involved, but there were rebels like Bill Jones and Henry Elliot, and right now Kirby could not tell how the majority would go.

It was wrong to divide these men into two sides that might be forced to fight each other, but it seemed to Kirby as his gaze swept the line of men in the fringe of the firelight that he had no choice. He would be struggling for his life as well as Dave Thorn's. More than that, a principle was at stake, a principle for which men had been giving their lives for centuries.

Kane stood on the opposite side of the fire from the others, moving away from Thorn and Kirby until he was about ten feet from them. He said pompously, "The court of the state of the Union is now in session for the purpose of trying David Thorn on a charge of high treason. Kirby Grant has volunteered to act as his attorney. You men will serve as a jury. It is understood that nothing which is said or done here tonight will ever be repeated to anyone outside of the Brotherhood upon pain of death."

"Your Honor," Norton broke in, "since we ain't sure how far away the bastards are who were supposed to get them horses, we ought to keep a guard south of the corral in case they surprise us. It's darker'n a bull's gut out there and they could—"

"We have Thorn's word that his men are as far south as Pueblo," Kane said harshly. "This agrees with information that was given to me. We are gathered here for the purpose of trying this man who has conspired all winter to take Colorado Territory into the Confederacy, and all of us have to bear the responsibility for what we do."

Norton stepped back, scowling and shaking his head. Kirby said, "Your Honor, your remarks are intended to prejudice the jury. It has not been proven at this time that David Thorn conspired—"

"The facts are known to every man here," Kane interrupted sharply. "Bill Jones was in the Criterion which is accepted to be the center of rebel activity in Denver. I believe he will be the only witness we need. Tell your story, Bill."

"That won't take long," Bill said. "As all of you know, I pretended to be a rebel sympathizer. I was inside the Criterion the morning the rebel flag was taken down from the Wallingford and Murphy store. I heard it said repeatedly by Thorn as well as others that he brought his horse herd to Colorado to use as mounts for rebel cavalry, and that when the right time came, they would occupy Denver."

Kane nodded, pleased. "I believe that is all the evidence we need. Do you gentlemen find the defendant guilty as charged?"

"Hold on," Kirby shouted. "This is ridiculous. I have a right to question the witness."

Kane faced him, his bearded face mockingly triumphant. "You can call it ridiculous or anything else you choose. The fact is that I will not be guilty of any maneuver that so clearly wastes time. Now what is the decision of the jury?"

"Guilty."

They said it together, every man who stood on the south side of the fire. They had come here to hang Dave Thorn, and Kirby wondered why Kane had even gone to the trouble of holding such a trial or of bringing the other men with him.

"David Thorn, you are found guilty of treason," Kane said. "As judge of this court, I sentence you to hang by the neck until dead, and may God have mercy on your soul." Kane turned to the men on the other side of the fire. "Now then, gentlemen, we have one other disagreeable duty to perform, the trial of one of our members. I accuse Kirby Grant of defiance, of insubordination, and of other crimes—"

"That's enough." Kirby drew his gun and jammed the muzzle against Kane's back. "You men saw the kind of trial that was given to Thorn. This is a lynching, and Kane is trying to give me the same treatment. I'm as loyal a Union man as any of you, but I also believe in law and order, not mob rule. I'm taking Thorn to Denver and turning him over to the legal authorities. If any of you try to stop me, I'll kill Martin Kane."

"Well, gentlemen," Kane said calmly, "I believe that Grant's gun in my back proves that he is guilty of defiance, of insubordination, and should be—"

Martin Kane never finished his sentence. Riders poured out of the darkness to the south, firing and yelling as they came. As Thorn jumped back from the fire, he shouted, "How do you like the sound of that rebel yell, Yanks? You'll hear it more than once before this fight's over."

Kirby plunged into the darkness and raced toward the corral gate, bullets snapping all around him. As he ran, he cursed Martin Kane's stupid stubbornness. This shouldn't have happened, and wouldn't have if Kane had listened to Phil Norton.

THIRTY

KIRBY had little idea how many men were making the attack, but judging from the yelling and shooting and thunder of hoofs, there must be fifty of them. They probably hoped to save Dave Thorn's life, but their main objective would be to open the corral gate and drive the horses south. That was the one maneuver Kirby must prevent.

As he ran through the darkness, he thought he had seen Martin Kane go down in the first hail of lead. He wondered, if he lived through this and if Martin Kane was still alive, what would happen. But he had no time for speculation. A rider was there at the gate ahead of him trying to open it. Kirby raised his revolver and fired. The horse whirled away as the rider slumped and slid out of the saddle.

For these first moments there seemed to be no pattern to the fighting, just wild yelling and shooting as horses raced by. Now Kirby put his back to the gate and stood there, his revolver at his side as he tried to make sense out of the chaotic action.

Someone must have kicked the wood off the fire. At least it had died down so there was very little light from it. In the darkness Kirby had no way of telling friend from enemy, and when he glimpsed a dim figure appearing in front of him, he raised his pistol and would have shot him down if the man hadn't yelled, "I'm Henry Elliot."

Kirby's finger eased its pressure on the trigger as he called, "I'm Kirby Grant."

A moment later Elliot was beside him, saying, "I figured somebody would be here. It's the horses they're after, not Dave Thorn. I've got a hunch he's dead anyhow."

Suddenly the attacking party converged on the corral, still yelling and firing. A bullet slapped into a log at the end of the gate, another splintered a board beside Kirby. He fired at the front rider and the horse veered off. Elliot was shooting, too, and Kirby had the impression that other men were running toward them, of Bill Jones and Phil Norton yelling, "Don't let 'em get the gate open."

A bullet stung Kirby's side. Another opened a gash in his left arm. He fired a third time at a rider in front of him whose horse was rearing. He missed and fired again, and this time the man rolled out of his saddle.

They were all over him then, a dozen of them on foot,

dim figures rushing up out of the darkness, intent on opening the corral gate and releasing the horses. Kirby slashed out with his gun, cracking one head as if it were an overripe melon. A descending gun barrel smashed against his left shoulder and drove him to his knees. He fell forward, his arms going around the legs of a man in front of him and bringing him into the dust.

They rolled over and over, Kirby hitting with his right fist when it was free, or kneeing the man in the crotch when he had a chance. They moved away from the gate as someone yelled jubilantly. "We've got 'em on the run." It sounded like Bill Jones's voice.

Kirby was on top now. He slugged the man with his right, a short, hammerlike blow that connected with the fellow's jaw. He went limp, and Kirby scrambled to his feet and wheeled toward the gate. He called, "Who's there?"

"That you, Kirby?" Bill asked.

"It's me," Kirby said.

"They've gone," Bill said. "The ones that could ride anyway. I reckon we took care of a few of 'em. You got one over there?"

"Yeah, I got one." Kirby felt along the ground, until he found his revolver, then a hand touched a man's foot, and he asked, "Who's this?"

"Henry Elliot, I think," Bill answered. "Sounded like he caught a slug just after I got here."

Kirby probed the darkness until he found the man's arm and tried to feel his pulse, but there was none. He rose and leaned against the gate. He said, "It's hell, Bill. I liked Elliot. He didn't want to come to Denver when I brought word to him. He told me he aimed to go prospecting the next day. That's how close I came to missing him."

"I liked Norton, too," Bill said. "He was beside me when we was headed for the gate, but all of a sudden he wasn't."

For a time they stood there, blood dripping down Kirby's left arm. His shoulder ached but apparently no bones were broken. He could not hear the receding hoof beats. The rebels had either stopped or kept going and now were too far away to be heard.

"We'll build up the fire and count noses," Bill said. "Some of us did a hell of a lot of fighting, but there was some others who didn't do nothing but hide their god-damned heads."

They threw wood on the fire as men began drifting toward it from the darkness. Someone said, "Here's Thorn. He's dead."

"I'll look at him, Kirby," Bill said. "No use of you seeing him." A moment later he added, "He's got three bullet holes in his back. I guess several of the boys were making sure the rebels didn't rescue him."

Phil Norton staggered toward the fire, holding his head. A bullet had sliced across his scalp, knocking him out. Henry Elliot was dead just as Kirby had been sure he was. Three dead rebels were found in front of the corral gate, but the man Kirby had knocked out with his fist had come to and slipped away.

"They may be back," Bill said, "so we'll stay awake and keep a guard at the gate, though I figure we gave 'em a hot enough reception that they'll stay away."

Martin Kane was not to be found. Some thought he had been taken prisoner. Bill went into the cabin with Kirby and put a tight bandage on his arm. They examined the shallow wound on his ribs and decided it wasn't enough to worry about. Then Bill looked at Kirby in the candlelight and asked, "What do you think about Martin?"

"He's not a prisoner," Kirby said. "We were having it too hot for them to be taking prisoners. When they gave up, they got out fast."

"That's what I figure," Bill said. "I believe he ran when the shooting started. Of course he knew he was to blame. If he'd kept Norton down there on the trail, the rebels wouldn't have surprised us. I don't think he could face us."

As much as Kirby disliked the man, he found it hard to believe that Kane would run when the shooting started. He still had the hazy memory of seeing Kane fall when the attack began, but he couldn't be sure, so he didn't say anything.

"I don't think he's going to try me like he was aiming to," Kirby said.

"No," Bill agreed. "I didn't believe he would go ahead with it, although he told me once that if you ever gave him trouble, that's what he'd do. He didn't have a chance of making it stick. His power wasn't as complete as he thought. He'd been living too long with his schemes and dreams." Bill scratched his jaw reflectively. "There's some kind of an old saying that total power totally corrupts. Martin's trouble was that he thought he had total power."

Looking at Bill in the thin light of the candle, Kirby realized how hard this night had been on him. He had followed Martin Kane's lead for a long time and had tried to believe in him, but he had been disillusioned at last.

There was a shovel and a pick in the cabin, and Bill ordered the men to start digging graves. When daylight came the rebels had not returned, so the guard was removed from the corral and a methodical search was started for Martin Kane. Within an hour Kirby found fresh tracks leading away from the river toward the top of the timbered ridge to the west.

"Bill," Kirby called, and waited until Bill Jones joined him.

For a time Bill studied the tracks. He followed them up the slope for another fifty feet, then turned to Kirby. "What do you make of it?"

"He ran," Kirby said flatly. "He was scared. All he could think of was to get away from the fighting. Looks like he fell down here, then he got up and went on." Kirby moved up the ridge to an open spot in the pine timber. "Here he fell down again, then it looks like he crawled on all fours."

Bill climbed up the slope to stand beside Kirby. He said, "Only he wasn't crawling. He was traveling like an animal till he got back on his feet." He pointed to long marks in the soft soil. "He was digging with his fingernails." He looked at Kirby. "Martin must have gone crazy."

"A man goes crazy for a while when he gets as panicky as Kane must have," Kirby said. "All he could think of was running away from where the bullets were flying, but up yonder somewhere he got over his panic. I wonder what he did then?"

Bill scratched his cheek. "I guess almost every man who ever lived has been up against this. I have."

"So have I," Kirby said. "When you get so you can think, you're ashamed and you wish to hell you could live the last hour over, but you know you can't, so you either go back and face whatever you ran from or you keep on running. Which is he going to do?"

"You've said he was a coward who got other men to do the fighting," Bill said thoughtfully, "but he can't do that any more. Besides being scared, he knows he's to blame for the surprise because he pulled Norton off the trail where he was standing guard." Bill shook his head. "He'll sure hate to face the music."

"He might be wounded," Kirby said. "Maybe he's holed up right here above us a little ways. Even if he's not wounded, he doesn't have a horse, there's no water up here, and he doesn't have any grub. He probably doesn't even have a rifle."

"So as soon as he starts thinking straight, he'll know he can't stay here," Bill said. "If he don't have enough sand in his craw to come back, what will he do? There's no place for him to run to."

They stood motionless for a moment, scanning the slope above them. The trees were scattered and there was almost no underbrush, but Kirby could see a number of boulders which would give a man adequate shelter.

Kirby took a long breath. He said, "I have never pretended to understand Kane, but I'm sure he's a devious man. I'm convinced he has worked for his own ends, and his devotion to what we believe in is only skin deep.

I may be doing him an injustice, but if I'm right, he'll try to go over to the rebels."

Bill was jolted by the thought. He scratched his cheek again, then he said thoughtfully, "I hate like hell to admit you might be right. I still believe he was sincere last fall when I came to Denver, and I believe he was changed by what has happened since then. In any case he may do what you're saying."

"Maybe he can't hurt us," Kirby said, "and maybe the rebels won't take him. They might kill him on sight, but he's a persuasive man at times."

"I don't like the notion of him telling 'em what secrets we still have," Bill said. "We'd better find him."

"It's my guess he's not far from here whether he's wounded or not," Kirby said. "If we're guessing right, I'd say he's hiding up yonder behind one of them rocks waiting for us to take the horses back to Denver, then he'll head south."

Bill moistened his lips. "I don't want to pull in the others unless we have to. There's a few men who are loyal enough, or maybe crazy enough to back him if he tells a good lie. We might wind up killing each other."

"Well then," Kirby said, "it's up to us. We'd better separate and angle up the ridge. If he starts shooting, we hit the dirt."

Bill nodded agreement. He turned and motioned as if there were a man far to his left. He shouted, "Tony, keep going straight to the top. Kirby and me are splitting up. We think Martin's up here ahead of us."

They moved away from each other and angled up the slope, Kirby's gaze moving from one rock to another, his right hand on the butt of his gun. He was within fifty yards of the top of the ridge when a gun roared above him, the bullet slicing through his coat under his right arm.

Kirby lunged toward a tall boulder that was ten feet ahead of him as Kane fired again, the slug kicking up dirt in front of him. "Let me alone," Kane screamed. "Go on back down to camp and let me alone."

Kirby heard Bill cut loose when he reached the boulder. He drew his gun and eased around the huge rock just as Kane started running downhill toward him. What possessed the man to do anything as foolish as this when he could have stayed under cover and been hard to flush out of his hiding place? Kirby had no time to figure out the reasons for Kane's behavior. Kane leveled his revolver and fired again, but he was slipping and sliding down the slope and his bullet was wild. Kirby yelled, "Throw your gun down."

But Martin Kane, his face a hideous mask of hatred, was beyond reason. He brought his revolver up for a third shot just as Kirby fired. The bullet knocked Kane down. He slid for ten feet on his face like a toboggan, starting a small slide of rocks and dirt, and then rolled over and over, coming to stop directly in front of Kirby.

Somehow he had held onto his gun. Now, with blood bubbling from the corners of his mouth, he lifted the revolver to fire again. It wobbled in his slack grip, and Kirby, taking a long step toward him, kicked it out of his hand.

Kane's fingers dug into the dirt as he tried to pull himself toward the gun, but he could not. He breathed, "Damn you, Grant! Why didn't you . . . stay . . . in . . . Kansas?"

He was dead by the time Bill Jones reached him. Bill looked down at the body, then at Kirby. "There's our leader," he said thickly. "I helped kill him. I was high enough to see him and I put my first bullet right in above his head. I thought maybe he'd throw his hands up and quit, but he had to try to get you."

Kirby nodded, but he wasn't sure whether that was true, or whether Kane wanted to die, but lacked the courage to put the muzzle of his gun to his head and pull the trigger. Kirby could not help comparing him to Dave Thorn, who had been a brave man, defiant to the last.

"I'll get a horse and tell the boys what happened," Bill said. "It had better be me than you, I think. You'd best stay here so some animal won't chew on him while I'm gone."

Kirby nodded. He climbed to the top of the boulder and sat down, watching Bill go down the slope. There were men, he knew, who, even after all that had happened, would blame Kirby for killing Martin Kane. They would remember that Kane had intended to try him last night for insubordination and defiance.

But when Bill returned with a horse to move Kane's body to camp, he said there would be no trouble, that not even Randy Curl could defend Kane's action of running away when the fight started. As he walked back to camp beside Bill Jones, who led the horse, the thought was in Kirby's mind that Martin Kane had been a paradox in death as he had in life.

The burying was finished by sundown. The corral gate was opened at dawn and the horse herd was started to Denver. The horses belonged to Liz Thorn and should be returned to her, Kirby said. No one argued with him about it.

When he stood in front of Liz that night, the light from the lamp in the living room falling on his face, she said, "He knew the chances he was taking. I didn't agree with him on a lot of things, Kirby, not even about coming to Denver, but it was something he had to do, so maybe this was the way he wanted to die."

"I'm sorry," Kirby said. "I respected him a lot."

"Don't be sorry," Liz said. "He would have used his gun to kill you without batting an eye if he'd felt it was necessary. That was how strongly he believed in what he was fighting for. It doesn't make much sense, does it, Kirby? You see, he was very fond of you."

As Kirby walked back to the Broadwell House, he thought that he would never know the truth about whether Dave Thorn or Martin Kane had sent John Deal to Boulder to kill him, and later had told Al McCoy to hire Duke Rome to try again. It was just as well. Liz might have told him if he'd asked her, but he didn't really want to know.

As it stood, he could respect the memory of Dave Thorn. He wanted to keep it that way. At times, he thought ruefully, it was hard, even painful, for a man to try to distinguish between his friends and his enemies.

THIRTY-ONE

KIRBY stood beside Suzy in front of the Tremont House, part of the wildly excited crowd that waited for the arrival of the newly appointed governor of the territory of Colorado, William Gilpin. This was May 27, 1861, almost three months after Colorado had been made a territory by an act of Congress, and only now, after a wait that had seemed endless, was a man arriving to take charge of the government.

Suzy looked up at Kirby and smiled, her hand squeezing his arm. They were, he guessed, just about the happiest newlyweds in the territory. She was as small and quick-tempered and pert as ever, and he loved her very much. She was the prettiest girl he had ever seen. He was certain of that, and he was proud of her.

She was wearing her hair in a chignon on her neck, and a small hat was tipped forward on her head, the ribbon quite wide and elegantly trimmed. She was neatly dressed in a pink, tight-fitting bodice and a full skirt trimmed with velvet braid.

"I love you," he said. "I'm proud to be your husband."

She smiled again, as if very sure of his love. She said, "I'm a little proud of you, too, darling."

Suddenly the crowd let out a whoop. A cloud of dust was visible now on the Platte River road. A short time later the swaying Concord coach and its hard-running team appeared in the street, and the people who had been inside the store now ran outside. Some of the men fired their revolvers into the air, and all of them cheered, Kirby along with the others.

Almost everyone was pleased that Gilpin had been chosen governor. He knew the West, he had been in what was now Colorado as early as 1844, and there was no doubt about his loyalty to the Union, a quality which particularly pleased Kirby. From now on there would be no need of men like Martin Kane, no need of spies, counterspies, and secret societies and their maneuvering. No, it would all be out in the open, with William Gilpin taking strong steps to keep Colorado in the Union.

The crowd kept whooping as Gilpin and his party worked their way into the Tremont House. Someone pressed a handbill into Kirby's hand. He glanced at it and saw that it told about the reception for the governor that evening. He showed it to Suzy who nodded and said, "We can't miss that, can we, husband?"

"No, wife," he said, and they both laughed as they turned toward their cabin.

Liz Thorn had sold her horses and the barn, and had taken an eastbound stage. Bill Jones had left for Kansas, saying he wanted to join a Kansas regiment and get into the fighting, but Kirby hadn't seen it that way. He had talked it over with Suzy, and they'd agreed they wanted to stay out here in Colorado, to grow with the territory and the state when it became a state. And to fight for it, Kirby said.

With William Gilpin sitting in the governor's chair, there would be a fight if the territory were invaded, or if men like Charley Harrison decided to take over by force. Some of the Southern sympathizers had left, but Harrison and a good many of the Bummers were still here. Either way, Kirby knew that men who believed in the Union as strongly as he did would be needed, and he could not agree with his brother-in-law that the proper thing to do was to return to Kansas.

As they walked along Front Street, Kirby thought of the many things that had happened since they'd left Linn County in Kansas almost a year ago. He wondered if he could have faced these months if he had known what lay ahead, but the Lord had showed His wisdom, Kirby thought, in keeping the veil drawn across the future. He had tasted the bitter as well as the sweet, and he guessed he wouldn't change much of anything even if he had his choice.

"Seems funny," he mused. "I guess a man walks along the edge of the unknown all the time."

Suzy glanced at him, startled. "My husband has turned philosopher," she said. "What brought that on?"

"I was thinking about how it's been since that first night we camped on Cherry Creek," he said. "Some of the most important fights are never mentioned in the history books, and folks never hear about them, but they're necessary just the same. The big fight hasn't started yet, but the things that have happened here and back in Kansas may have helped decide the way it's going to turn out. One thing's sure. The big fight's going to get started mighty soon. I guess that's the only way the issue will ever be settled."

"You'll be in the big fight," she said a little bitterly. "So will Bill. But are you sure it will settle the issue? Have the big fights ever settled anything?"

"Now who's the philosopher?" he asked, smiling.

"Well, have they?" she asked. "You'll save the Union. Maybe the slaves will be freed, but is that going to solve all the problems? Will the white people say to the Negroes that you can vote and hold office and we love you because the North has freed you by killing a lot of us?"

"No," he admitted, "it won't solve all the problems. I

guess we'll never see the day when all the problems have been solved. It would be a dull world if they were." He stopped her and looked down at her face. "I wanted to kiss you back there in front of the Tremont House. Now I'm going to do it."

When he let her go a moment later and they walked on, his arm around her, she said a little breathlessly, "Kirby, aren't you ashamed to kiss me right out here on Front Street?"

"Why no," he said. "I'm not ashamed a bit. I'd just as soon kiss you on Front Street as anywhere."

Center Point Publishing
600 Brooks Road • PO Box 1
Thorndike ME 04986-0001 USA

(207) 568-3717

US & Canada:
1 800 929-9108